I0547833

SEX MACHINE

By
Shepard Mead

SEX MACHINE
by Shepard Mead

Published by Pulp Culture Press

44 Race Street
San Jose, CA 95126

www.pulpculturepress.com

ISBN: 978-1-59362-328-9

POD Edition

I was beginning to get that lightheaded feeling again, and the one beer didn't have a thing to do with it. "Maybe you don't understand," I said. "We're trying to find out what color the public favors."

"The hell with the public. Now, I don't mean that unkindly, sonny. I mean, what business you got makin' an average color that everybody ought to like and havin' a machine turn out a hundred million of 'em? You trying to make everybody use the same flavor toothpaste?"

EDITORS NOTES

The Sex Machine is not a book about a machine used for sex, nor is it even about a machine at all. Instead, it is a novel based on polls of public opinion. What might happen if a single person could predict public opinion, or at least the results of a public opinion poll, simply by being presented with the questions and telling you what he liked? The idea is that this one person, someone named MacInnes, had a taste that matched the average American and that instead of spending time and money on public opinion polls all you had to do was present your question to MacInnes and boom his answers would match those of any poll.

In short, **The Sex Machine** is about polls, poll takers, and the power they had over what we saw, read, ate, listened to, and everything else that impacted our lives. As I was writing this, I had finished listening to an interview with Mark Cuban. As he talked about the modern-day internet and what we saw and were pointed to, he said, "Whoever controls the Algorithm controls the world." This is the plot/scheme of **The Sex Machine**. The character MacInnes was a walking talking algorithm generator and, through his manipulation of public opinion polls could steer this country in any way he wanted, if he wanted to, which apparently he did not.

Initially published in 1946 under the title *The Magnificent MacInnes* and written by Shepherd Mead, who would later find fame with his novel *How To Succeed In Business Without Really Trying*, the book you hold in your hands is a repackaged version of that book was retitled **The Sex Machine** and was billed as "A Ribald Novel". What makes the novel "Ribald,"? I have no idea. Ultimately, there are some scenes where sexy women cavort around in bikinis, and then there is a search for the most beautiful woman in America., but that's about it. Those scenes seemed a bit out of place, and how it reads to me is that the original publisher, who no doubt owned the manuscript, decided to take a few of their slower-selling titles, add some titillating details, and repackage it as a book that would appeal to the prurient interest.

I, of course, have no proof of that other than this is how it reads to me. What I will say is that in a couple of spots in the book, there are some unfortunate references to rape in the book, as in one place where one of the characters says, "There comes a time in every man's life where he needs to rape his wife."

This was shocking for me to read, and honestly, I sort of felt like it was maybe one of the things put in by someone trying to make the book sexier for this edition, someone who had no idea what they were doing. At first, I thought about changing the word "rape" to "ravish". However, ravishing is still sort of a cleaned-up way of referring to forcing yourself on someone. As I read the passage repeatedly, I realized how out of place either word was and that it most likely did not appear in the original manuscript. So I just eliminated it, and it changed absolutely nothing about the book, the characters, or how they acted in the book, and kept the man who uttered the phrase a sympathetic character.

The other reason this was shocking was that this book is generally better written than some of the other examples of the Pulp genre that I have come across. I have to admit that the salacious title attracted me to it, and I expected a great and goofy send-up of 1940s sexual mores. What I got was something that you could probably do a version of today using AI as the motivation for the pollsters to try and game the information-gathering system.

The cover image is signed as Xela, which a little research reveals was a pen-name for famed comic book cover artist Alex Schomburg, whose work graced covers for Captain America, Sub-Mariner, and more for Timely Comics, the predecessor of Marvel Comics. The work signed as Xela featured a different look than his comics work and appeared on pulp novels and the lije through the 1940s. This particular cover was scanned from a very poor reproduction of the original and had a very nasty dot pattern in it, which we could not get rid of, so using upscaling tools at our disposal, we resized the image, which made the two girls on the front look okay, but details were lost in other parts of the cover.

The interior images are a combination of clipart and AI-generated art meant to add value and enjoyment to this edition of the book. In doing the AI generation, I decided not to replicate Schomberg's look as himself or as Xela but just shoot for some standard illustrations.

So, there you have it, The Sex Machine. Not the book the publishers wanted you to think it was (they never are) but it is still a semi-interesting look into our past.

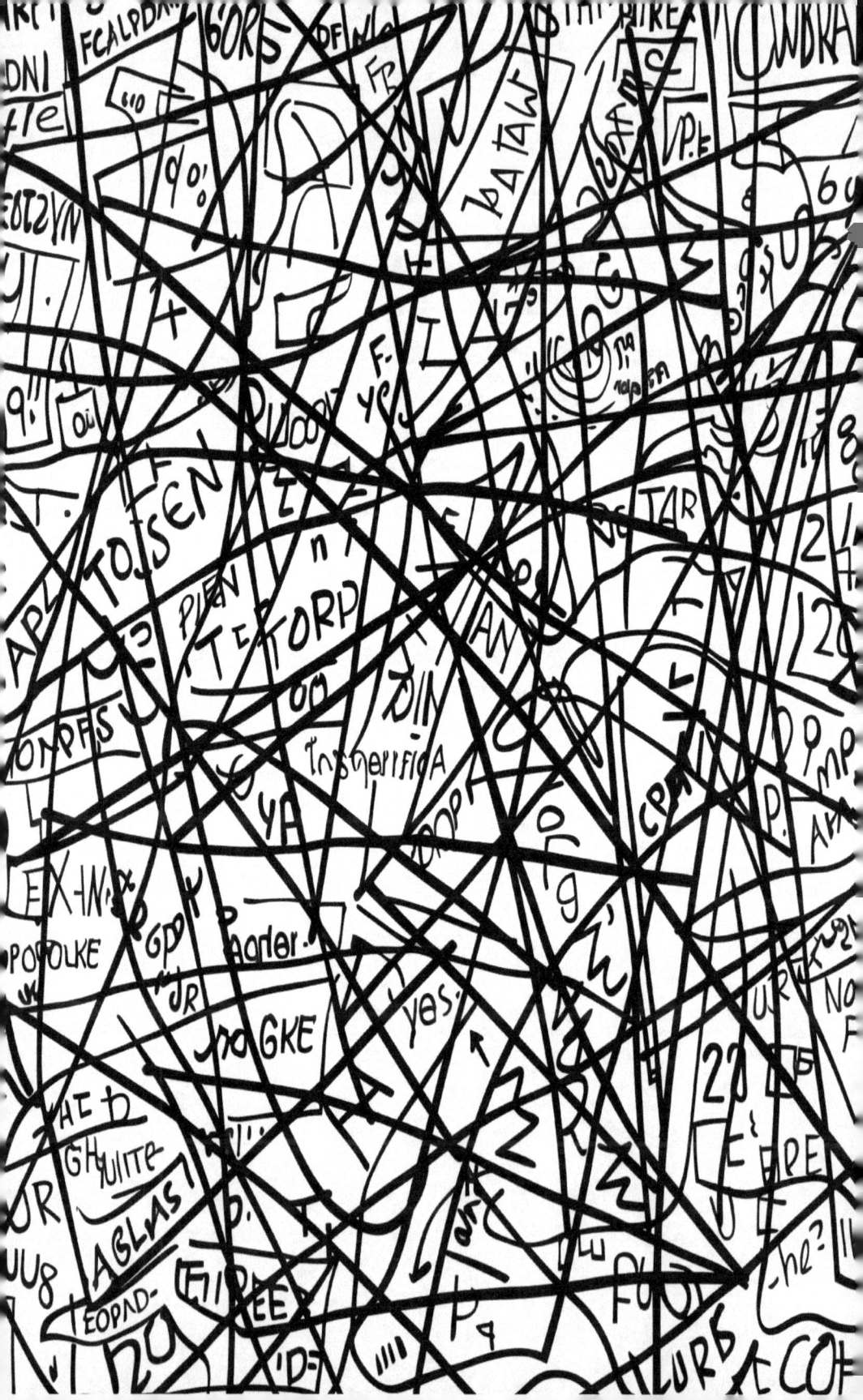

CHAPTER ONE

It may be hard to believe now, but if you think back, you'll realize that just six months ago, you had never even heard of MacInnes. Of course, you might say that six months before Hiroshima, you had never heard of the Bomb. But if you hadn't, you were in the minority, for a great many people had, including the ten million-odd readers of Amazing Comics, Superman, and a dozen other cartoon and pulp fiction magazines. And yet, as that committee from the University of Chicago stated, MacInnes was "potentially ten times more dangerous than all the military ramifications of nuclear physics." You may say that's an exaggeration since MacInnes never really hurt any thing or anybody, but on the whole, I think it may have been true.

I realize you may be one of those who were deeply offended by the Chicago statement. So many believed (and some still be believe) that MacInnes was the only hope of mankind. There were and I suppose still are-all, degrees of feeling about him. To some, he was a crackpot; to others, an amazing phenomenon; and to still others, the Hand of God or the sign of the arrival of the Millennium. He even became a deity to that little group in California, and today, you can see the half-finished temple of stucco and glass brick on Sunset Boulevard. (They stopped work on it the day after the great Christmas collapse.)

But almost as amazing as MacInnes himself was this fact: he had been living among us all these years, with all his powers, like the uranium that has been sleeping in the earth. I discovered him that spring, almost by accident. It began on a wet March day about a year ago. I was sitting at my desk going over surveys. Polls, you know. They called me a "tabulation supervisor." I was sort of a glorified clerk who checked the figures that came in. (I was one result of the Scientific Re-evaluation that followed Black Wednesday last November - Black Wednesday that smashed Standard Research Associates and forced its merger with Advertising Idea Research to form Standard-Idea, Inc.)

Outside, on Lexington Avenue, the taxis were jammed and bleating, and inside there were mushroom beds of drying umbrellas, baggy pants, and spotted nylons. Diana came into my office. Well, I called it an office. It was a steel and frosted-glass cubicle with the dimensions of a junior size pool table.

"I got a question," Diana said.

"Be right with you," I told her, giving my slide rule a final push.

"How do you want this tabulation typed? Up and down or sideways?"

I looked at the paper. With Diana, it was always hard to keep looking at the paper, but I did. Diana was built like one of those Esquire cartoons, busty, curvy, and long-legged. "Well," I said, "maybe the titles up and down, like this, and the opinions listed across the top."

"Okay."

"How did they come out?" I told myself I really cared how they came out. It didn't matter having Diana there, bending bustily over my desk.

"Macbeth came out third," she said. We were testing titles for a movie. We tested anything and took a poll on it. We had radio ratings, like Hoopers, and we'd get you figures on what people thought about anything: the readership of an advertisement, the title of a book, the color of your cornflakes. This was a movie version of Macbeth. The tabulation showed that Night of Madness was favored by twenty-eight percent. The Walking Woods by twenty-two percent, Macbeth by eigh teen percent, and others trailing. The Road to Dunsinane had been the big favorite in early test areas, but we discovered in time that this was just because those questioned believed the cast would include Bob Hope and Bing Crosby.

"Hmmmmm, third place for Macbeth," I said. "That's pretty ' good. Think what the old boy could have done with our modern facilities."

Diana's gum missed two beats, as it always did when she was deciding whether or not I was kidding. "Ha," she said, not committing herself. "I'll type this up." She winked and gathered up the papers. Diana's wink was strictly a Hiyah or Okay wink, sexy with her long lashes and mascara, but not meant to be, and was used for both males and females. Her mother had probably told her she had certain obvious advantages, and not to go throwing them around loosely.

"Uh, Diana-" I began, my hormones beginning to percolate. What would she like? A movie? Roseland? A nightclub?

"I almost forgot, Mr. Beecher," she said, very business-like. "Dr. Temple called. Wants you to call him back."

"Oh. Thanks." That was my trouble. I appealed to the intellectual type, the true heart in the flat but honest breast. I was shorter than the fellows who occasionally came to meet Diana, my hair was sort of bristly, and I wore pret-ty heavy glasses. I grabbed the phone, watching Diana walk out, swaying her shoulders back and forth like a football halfback. Maybe she thought that was business-like, too.

Temple asked me to come in. He had an office with real walls, and a secretary all his own, not a share-cropping arrangement like mine with Diana, who was mostly a tabulating typist. When I went in, Temple was looking at a chart on his desk. He looked at it for several seconds and then suddenly looked up, startled. Maybe it was an act. We could never figure it out. Temple was about ten years older than I, in his upper thirties somewhere. He was a Ph.D. in Applied Psychology and a former assistant professor at Yale. He went around the office in kind of a trance, with his oversized head bent down toward the floor and his heavy black hair falling over his forehead. People said he got his job because of a thesis he wrote on radio audience measurement. Like a lot of high-voltage solitary thinkers, he was slapped into an administrative job. It suited him about as much as being an end man in a minstrel show.

"Oh, uh, hello, Fred," he said to me. "Did you call?"

"Oh. Oh, that." He looked under the chart and found a stack of papers. "Have a look at these surveys." The surveys were part of a nationwide test we were making for a cosmetic company that wanted to know what perfume people liked in a face cream. A routine job. Our researchers asked people to smell and compare four different scents.

"I thought this was already tabulated," I said. "Gardenia won."

"That's right. But we were checking back over the reports for a breakdown by age groups, and this one looked suspicious." I thumbed through the reports, looking at the "Estimated Age" spaces, where the field workers wrote down their own estimates.

"These look phony," I said, "unless the surveys were all made at a college and an old folks' home. Half of them say 'about 20' and the other half 'about 70.' "

"It was a door-to-door operation in Astoria."

"Then it's a phony, all right. We should have caught it the first time through." I knew it was an old trick, and so did Temple. Sometimes a field worker was lazy or dishonest and would simply make up the answers instead of doing actual interviews. It was rare because we tried to take great care in picking our researchers. We had young men and women, house wives, college students, sometimes teachers, hundreds of them, scattered all over the country.

"Well, check into it, will you?" Temple said. "See how much It will affect the totals if we throw out this batch."

"Okay. And I guess I'd better go back and check this researcher's other interviews."

"You may have to fire her."

"Is it a her?"

"I don't know. The name's M. L. Maddox."

"Maybe Maddox got sick and just tried to bluff through one survey."

"Well, check up and let me know, Fred."

"Okay." I went out, taking the surveys with me. At the door, I looked back. Temple was in his trance again, looking straight ahead and far away. Back at my desk, I compared Maddox's results with the national figures. If they were about the same, then throwing out this set wouldn't affect the national results.

"We're lucky," I said to Temple on the phone. "Maddox's figures are almost exactly the same as the national preferences. Gardenia, lavender, mixed fragrance, and violet, in that order."

"Hmmmmm," said Temple. "Pretty good proof that the surveys were faked. All the other New York reports gave lavender first. Gardenia went ahead in the Middle West."

"Maybe that just proves M. L. Maddox is from the Middle West."

"Possibly."

"I'll check her file now," I said.

"Her file?"

"I don't know yet. But I can't imagine a man picking gardenia."

Diana brought me M. L. Maddox's file. Margaret Lane Maddox. People probably called her Peggy. Born in Baltimore. (I checked the Maryland preference at this point, and it was violet, with gardenia second.) Twenty-four years old. Two years at Columbia University. Previous job, receptionist. That meant she must be pretty good-looking. She was hired by my predecessor, but I was the one who would have to fire her if the other surveys looked suspicious. I hate firing people.

Diana was in with an armful of Miss Maddox's surveys by this time. Flipping through them quickly, I noted one batch asked for the names of those interviewed. According to Miss Maddox, the population of Washington Heights included Silas Marner, Anna Livia Plurabelle, and Leonardo da Vinci, all of them seventeen years old. This was statistically possible but rather unlikely.

In the next group, occupations were listed. Most of them were safely filled in with "Housewife," including one who was described in another blank as "Male." However, there were two bareback riders, a human fly, three deep-sea divers, and one witch out of a sample of a hundred and twenty-three. We really should have checked those surveys more closely. I called Diana and asked her to get Miss Maddox in here first thing in the morning.

I was getting worried now. Maddox was lucky on the four perfumes, but how many surveys had she spoiled? I took one batch of questionnaires testing names for breakfast food. There were fifteen names — things like "Whete," "Strongo," and "Crispettes" — and the people questioned were supposed to check the ones that appealed to them most.

I called Diana and asked her to make up two tabulations: first, the national preferences in these names; second, Miss Maddox's list, in order. Then I lit a pipe and watched the rain come down. I would have paced back and forth but didn't have a pacing room. One step in any direction, and I'd hit a partition. Knowing now what Macinnes was and what he did, you can guess what was going to happen. But if I'd told you all this before you heard of him, you might say, "Those are statistics; they're numbers on paper." And you might wonder what they had to do with you.

But even before Macinnes, we'd started the first decade of the Poll Age. Even then, it was the polls that determined almost everything you bought and heard on the radio, who you voted for, and, partly even read: the color of your clothes and your pudding and your face cream, the shape of your car, the titles and even the stories of your movies, and the content of your magazines (if you read the ones made of smooth paper). They shaped your political platform and often picked your candidate. Then, sometimes, they even helped defeat him with overconfidence because you forgot that the poll was the final verdict in everything but elections.

All these things poured from the fountainhead of questionnaires, giving you tomorrow what you wanted yesterday, ad infinitum. It was a composite leader, leading in an average direction, which is no direction. You forgot that people could be reached and led by individual good taste and intelligence, that people could tire of the cliche and welcome the original.

But I didn't realize all that as I sat there watching the rain. If I thought of it at all, I suppose I thought that I was a cog in some sort of machine for pure democracy. But mostly, I just thought of it as a living and within the law. Diana came in, walking with that halfback swagger of hers, and put the tabulations on my desk, all typed crisp and clean. She had even found time to put a fresh coat on her face, includ ing a gob of that near-purple lipstick she used. She could put it on just the way she did her work. Fast and business-like.

I saw at a glance that Maddox's list was in exactly the same order as the national one, from Vitawheat (number one) to Wheatsie-Puddy (number fifteen). The odds against doing that by chance must be twenty million to one.

"Quick!" I shouted. "Get me her other surveys!"

"Here they are," Diana said, winking. "I thought you'd want the others after you saw that one."

I could count on Diana. I looked at the first set of figures, which Diana had clipped to the national results. "They're the same!"

"They all are," said Diana.

"All of them?"

"Well, almost all. There was one. Back in November. According to Miss Maddox, Mr. Truman was supposed to--"

"That's enough!" I said.

"She must work in a very average community."

"She worked all over. The Bronx, Queens, Manhattan — all over, And New York is definitely not average for the country. Look, Diana. I want you to get her in here first thing in the morning."

"I already called her. She's coming in at ten. She sounds nice." Diana went out, leaving me to stare at a cold pipe held in a trembling hand. Even the Lexington Avenue bus couldn't knock Miss Maddox out of my head.

"Step back inna bus, please, step back inna bus," the driver kept shouting. And I, jammed wriggling and dripping between a three hundred-pound woman with four packages and a soggy laborer who smelled of wet wool and garlic, still kept thinking, "Ho did she do it?" Two blocks past my stop, I came to, beat my way out, and walked through the rain to our old brownstone.

I went up the three flights of squeaking stairs, breathing mostly through my mouth. I could never get used to the hall way smell of that old house. It was a stale, musty smell, like a week-old baked potato. My roommate, Colter, was home, and had been most of the day. Colter Fleming. In fact, it was even W. Colter Fleming. We'd been in school together. He was a few years older, taller, and much heavier, with a round reddish face and straight black hair that fell in front of his eyes. When I came in, he was in shirt sleeves, with his collar open, walking up and down in front of the radio, which was tuned in to one of those "ideas" shows. You know, the questions, or the contestants, spin round and round, and everybody wins a house and lot and a ticket to Hollywood.

"You're not listening to that, are you?" I asked.

"Shhhhh." He listened carefully while the announcer read a set of rules that was as long as the Constitution of the United States. "What's the rating?" he asked me.

"How do I know? I don't even know the name of it."

"'Ask me a Double.' See, the gimmick is, there are two guys with questions, and-"

"Okay. I'll look it up for you tomorrow."

"The important thing is the gimmick. The twist is, there are these two guys and-"

"All I need is the name."

"Beech, I don't get you. Pushing around those lousy numbers all day for a measly sixty bucks a week, when do you know what the guy who thought of that simple little gimmick is pulling down every week?"

"No, do you?"

"On this particular one, no. In general, yes. All this guy does is think up this little twist. So he calls himself a package producer. He produces package shows, get it? He hires a couple of jolly announcers or emcees, he gets a four or five-piece band, and he sells the whole show to some advertising agency for maybe two thousand bucks a week. And it costs him a thousand, maybe. That's a thousand bucks a week, pure gravy — for doing nothing!"

That was Colt, all right. The promoter. Still living on a few dollars that his father sent him every week and trying to get the big Angle, the Twisteroo that would put him into the big money. He had already had five different schemes, but he hadn't made a dollar yet.

"What's in the house for food?" I asked.

"Let's eat out, Beech. You've got a couple of bucks you can lend me, haven't you?"

I looked i the cabinet. We had a two-burner stove and an icebox that would hold six bottles of beer. It was in a sort of "dressing room" roughed out of wallboard, jig-sawed around the ornate moldings, squatting there across the old scarred pattern of inlaid flooring. Our whole "apartment" was jig-sawed that way, like a plush-lined egg crate fitted with cardboard dividers — our whole "two and a half rooms" made out of one big one. But they couldn't take away the high ceilings, not till they figured a way to put in double-decker apartments, like those new trains.

"How do you like chili and tamales?" I said.

"We've got two cans."

"Why is it always chili and tamales? I'm beginning to grow a sombrero."

"I don't get paid till tomorrow. We'll make a martini first."

SEX MACHINE

"There isn't any vermouth."

"There's some old sherry. It'll do."

"Poverty isn't becoming to me," said Colt, getting down the bottles. "I'm a darling of luxury. Tomorrow, if my check comes, I'll buy you a dinner." He would, too. He'd get a check from his dad in Chicago, and he'd be generous as hell until it ran out. Maybe it was a good thing his family had money. And maybe not. He had his father's example to prove that a long shot can come through.

Colt was exactly like his father, right down to his unlimited energy for avoiding conventional work. Colt's father had believed that one Good Idea could make a man's fortune. He had successively tried a scheme having to do in some way with those paper rolls for player pianos, a soft drink, and a pimple remover. He had finally cashed in modestly on a licorice-flavored laxative called Lic-O-Lax, which he manufactured in Chicago. Irritating the intestines of America had netted him perhaps a quarter of a million dollars. So you couldn't tell Colt he was wasting his time playing the angles. He had seen it happen.

Colt started mixing the martinis, if you could call them that, in an old, cracked water pitcher, swirling them around with a kitchen tablespoon. "Have we got any olives?" he asked.

"No. Use lemon peel," I said. I was putting on dry clothes, some old slacks and moccasins.

"Hello, old friend," Colt said, getting out the lemon. It was naked and white, having been stripped before to make other martinis.

"Maybe we could get it retreaded."

"It might be simpler," he said, "if we could just learn to drink gin."

I felt better with the drink inside me. As I warmed up the tamales, I could listen philosophically to Colt, who was facing the fact that his latest project seemed to be doomed. It had something to do with comic books and the promotion of dolls and gimcracks to go with it. "It's still a good idea," he said. "All I needed was a little
Capital."

The first time I heard him say that, I asked him why he didn't ask his father. He wouldn't. It was a point of honor with him. He wanted it to be his own idea, his own promotion, and his own profits. "You might," I said, "try doing an honest day's work. Tomorrow I have to fire an investigator. I'll hire you. Thirty five a week."

"A dishwasher makes more."

"We know that. That's why the company requires at least two years of college. Nobody with two years of college would wash dishes. They have to take less."

"You ought to specify Ph.D.'s. You could get them for thirty. You know, Beech," he added, as we sat down to our tamales, "your business reminds me of the guy who pulls the switches that light up the mutuel board at the race track. If he could know what he knew just a few minutes earlier, he'd be a millionaire in a week."

I stopped a forkful of tamales in mid-air. I could see the survey results of M. L. Maddox, right on the button, right down the line. Pure coincidence, maybe, or a trick. I'd find out in the morning how she did it.

"What's the matter?" Colt asked.

"I just thought of something funny that happened in the office today. Just a statistical freak. Not important."

"You watch yourself, Beech, or someday you'll be a statistical freak. And not important."

"Could be," I said, lighting into the chili and the tamales.

CHAPTER TWO

Look at those names, Miss Maddox!" I said, trying my best to glare executively across the desk. "Silas Marner! Leonardo da Vinci!"

"Oh, did I put those down?" She smiled. Unashamed. Almost proud. She was pretty in an undramatic but soft and pleasant way. Dark-brown hair and big friendly eyes that reminded me of an Irish setter I used to know.

"There is, of course," I went on, "an outside possibility that they do live in Washington Heights. But they don't have telephones. I looked."

"Oh, I didn't get them out of the phone book. I made those up." She said it proudly, rather creatively.

"You made them up!" I was trying to be indignant. Mean while, the wild, un-tamed part of me was saying, "Nice construction. Almost as nice as Diana's, but she doesn't make such a point of it. A girl with a body like that shouldn't wear tweed suits."

"I did use the telephone book for a long time, but it just seemed so stodgy."

"We certainly don't want stodgy reports," I said, a strange never-never-land feeling sweeping over me like a ground fog. "Miss Maddox," I said slowly, "you're not supposed to make things up in these surveys. You just ask people and write the answers down."

"Well, it just didn't seem to work out for me," she said in her pleasant, slightly Southern accent.

"You mean you tried it our way first?"

"I gave it every chance, I really did. I asked, and I asked, and I just couldn't get the right answers. I never found any average people.

"How do you know?"

"They printed one of the surveys in the paper. That one about Mr. Truman and the Russians a long time ago. And my people were all wrong. It must have thrown you all off."

"Miss Maddox," I said, trying to be patient, "all areas can be different. New York is sometimes different from Kansas or from California. That's why we have dozens of people all over the country. We have tabulators, and adding ma-chines, and slide rules, and — "

SEX MACHINE

"It's so hard the way you do it. And you know, I couldn't think of a better way myself for a long time, so I shouldn't blame you."

"Thank you," I said. I had an almost uncontrollable urge to break my slide rule into little pieces of kindling and make a bonfire on my desk.

"You see," she said, "it might not have happened at all if I hadn't had the grippe that day."

"What day?"

"Let me see." She started to count back on her fingers. "It couldn't have been around October 15, could it?" She finished counting. "Why, yes!" she said, beaming. "Could you tell the difference?"

I looked back through the surveys. Eleven of them. Every single one agreed exactly with the national results. Beginning on October 15.

"Yes," I said weakly. "I could."

"Well, with the grippe, you can see that I couldn't go out in the rain. It was raining that day. And besides, I was worried. I'd come in here one day and looked at some of the other results, and mine were all wrong. So I decided to try the other way and see what happened.

"You began making them up?"

"You mean the names? I had to make that part up, yes."

"You didn't make it all up?"

"Oh, no. Well, I handed them in when they were all ready, and I just dropped around the office a few weeks after that to see if it was any better. Well, it was. All my answers seemed to be just about right."

"They were exactly right," I said, my hands shaking.

"Well, you might have written me a letter or something. Nobody said a thing. I'll bet my answers were the best ones you had."

"They certainly were."

"I know you're busy. It was awfully nice of you to ask me to come in just to tell me that."

"Yes, yes," I said. "Even if it is a little late."

"Oh, that's all right!"

"Just sit there very quietly, Miss Maddox," I said. "I want you to tell me how you got the answers to all these questions."

She just smiled at me very pleasantly. "What's the matter?" I asked.

"I'm sorry, Mr. Beecher. I just can't tell you."

"You mean you don't know how you do it?"

"Oh, yes."

"What do you do?"

"I don't do anything."

"Who does?"

"I'm sure he wouldn't want me to tell you."

"Who's *he*?"

"I shouldn't have said that."

"But there is someone who works with you on this?" I felt that I was getting red. I knew I shouldn't try to grill her this way, but nothing was reasonable now. There could have been hobgoblins on the adding machines and tabulations written in three-four time with a boogie beat.

She stood up. "It was very nice of you to see me, Mr. Beecher," she said.

"Just a minute." I was on my feet, swaying stupidly but trying to think fast. "I have a special assignment for you."

" What assignment? I hoped I could find something." She smiled and sat down again.

"I'm sorry I was so curious," I said. "The main thing is that your answers were very good." I was glad Temple couldn't hear me.

"Thank you."

"You might be a big help to us in a quick survey of a trial balloon. How long would it take you to get me the answers to about a dozen questions on, say, two hundred questionnaires?" Done conventionally, it was several days' work.

"I could have them for you tomorrow."

SEX MACHINE

"Well, I really have two problems. The other is about the same size. It would help to find how many she could do in a day."

"I think I could have that tomorrow, too."

"You couldn't do three?"

"I don't think I should ask him to" She stopped. "I think three might be too much for one day," she finished.

"I see. You don't want to impose on your friend." She smiled. But that was all. She just smiled. I told her that the material wasn't ready and asked her to come back after lunch.

When she left my office, I called Diana and asked her to find out if we had any preliminary sets of surveys we were going to give to our regular researchers during the next week or two. There was one all ready to mail out and another that would be off the mimeograph machine before noon.

I knew Miss Maddox would have to do her work sometime between two that afternoon and the following morning. And if she was going to see "him" during that time, it shouldn't be too difficult to find out who he was. My first thought was to follow her when she left the office and shadow her all afternoon and, if necessary, all evening until I located the man who was helping her. I fancied myself as a cool but scientific Philip Marlowe, blending myself adroitly into the shadows, armed only with my wits and a portable slide rule.

But I knew it wouldn't work. No matter how well I acted like the hero in the second feature, I had a vague feeling that there might be something to tailing someone that wasn't shown at Loew's Lexington. And besides, she'd recognize me in any thing short of a suit of full armor.

I picked up the classified phone book, the big red one that weighs as much as a Shetland pony and turned to Detectives. There might be one or two listings. Try it sometime. You'll never feel safe again. There were about five pages full of advertisements. There must be more detectives in New York than there are plumbers. Investigations. Wire-tapping. Shadowing. Payroll service. One big display said that the Clark Investigating Service was run by a former lieutenant of detectives in the New York Police Force. That was, for me-honest, reliable, and probably unimaginative. If they found a gold mine, they wouldn't know it.

I dialed the number, and their operator gave me an extension. This fellow who answered was obviously using one of those hush-hush devices on his mouthpiece, one of those gadgets that keep people in your office from hearing what you're saying and make you sound as though you were talking from the bottom of a pickle barrel. The fellow was business-like, told me the job would cost about thirty-five dollars, and said he'd be in my office in an hour.

Diana came in with word that Temple had been trying to reach me while I was busy.

Temple! I knew I ought to call him right back. "I'll call him," I said to Diana.

"Did you fire her?" she said.

"Not exactly."

"What does that mean?"

"You'll see."

Diana winked at me in her wholesome way and sashayed out, the shoulders bouncing.

The phone rang again. I got up and went to the washroom. If I didn't answer, the call would go to Diana, and she'd be back with the message, and wondering what was the matter with me. But I knew it was Temple again, and I knew he'd ask me the same thing: "Did you fire her?" I had to think up a stall.

I sat for some time, thinking, and then went back to my office. Diana was in right after me. "It's Temple again. You'd better call him."

"I'll go in," I said. Temple was bending over a desk full of figures when I went in, but this time he was in no trance. He stood up when he saw me, and I couldn't help remembering he was a football player and a heavyweight boxer in college. I had to look up at him in spite of the way he hung his big shaggy head.

"What did you find out about Maddox?" he asked.

"Very bad," I said.

"How many surveys will it affect?"

"None."

"None?"

"Knocking out her results won't affect the averages. She was right."

"How many do you think she faked?"

"Eleven."

"How many were right?"

"Eleven."

"It isn't possible."

"I know."

"Did you fire her?"

I tried to keep my voice steady. "No," I said.

"Why not?"

"I think she's part of a ring."

"A ring?"

"I mean, she must be in touch with our other people in somehow! How else would she be so right?"

"Mmmmmm."

I knew it was nonsense, but it might seem logical. "Who knows? They may be rigging all our results."

"That's fantastic."

"Her results are fantastic."

"Mmmmmm."

I knew I had him there. "On the other hand," I said, "there may be nothing to it at all. But I thought I'd hang on to her. I'm going to give her the new picture survey and the toothpaste job."

"Mmmmmm."

"If she's working with somebody, we'll find out who it is."

"How?"

"Follow her."

"Yourself?"

"No." I knew this part was a chance, but at this stage in the game, I was willing to take a chance to get the company to pay the detective. "I thought I'd hire a detective. She said she could do both jobs by tomorrow morning."

"That's ridiculous."

"Hiring the detective?"

"No, doing both those jobs by tomorrow morning."

"That's why I want to have her followed."

"Do you know a good detective agency?"

"I've already called one. Clark Investigating. They estimate the job will cost thirty-five dollars. Want me to go ahead with it?"

"Try it this once. Might be good insurance."

"All right." I went out, pleased that I'd saved thirty-five dollars. You can say it was a false economy, but remember, on that March day I hadn't yet heard of Macinnes, and thirty-five dollars was a lot of money, more than half a week's pay. About half an hour later, the detective arrived. He was a large man with a short haircut, a dark blue shirt, and a New York accent.

"It isn't a very exciting case," I said. "Not a murder or any thing like that."

He nodded. "Clark, don't handle murders, mister. You get that for free, like parking tickets."

"I guess you got your fill of that on the police force."

"Clark was on the force, mister, not me. I been in this racket for fifteen years."

"No murders in all that time?"

"Once we was working around the fringe on one of a divorce case."

I was disappointed. "I just want you to follow a girl and give me a report on where she's been and the people she's talked to."

"Where do I pick her up?"

"In our reception room about two o'clock. Her name is Maddox. She'll come in to see me, and I'll come back out to the reception room with her when she goes."

"Okay."

"Remember, she isn't a criminal. I don't want her roughed up in any way."

I might just as well have accused International Business Machines of not Thinking. He was hurt and a little insulted.

"Mister," he said, "if everything goes okay she won't even know she's being tailed."

"Good."

I signed a paper, gave him Miss Maddox's address and my phone numbers, both at the office and at home and said goodbye to him. It must have been several minutes later that Diana came in. "Thinking?" she said.

I jumped. I must have jumped six inches. "Oh. Yes, I guess so."

"Gee. You're getting more like Temple every day."

"I was just thinking about the Maddox situation."
"So was I. How does she do it? What's the trick?"

"I don't know," I said. But as Diana went out, leaving on my desk the two advance surveys, I couldn't help thinking that perhaps I would know, and sooner than she thought.

I had asked Miss Maddox to come in at ten the next morning, and she was right on time. It was a fine sunny day, and she was wearing a bright green hat and a gay expression.
"You know," she said, "on a day like this, I feel downright homesick for Baltimore. Here they are, Mr. Beecher, both the surveys."

"Thank you."

"I hope you'll forgive me. I didn't fill them all out, but the main results are there. You said not to bother to make up the names this time."

"That's right." Yes, I had said not to make up the names, but I hadn't said not to fill out any of the surveys. "But look," I added, "do you mean that you've got the results without filling in the questionnaires?"

"I just didn't have the time. You said yourself it was asking a good deal."

"Yes. Yes, it was." I was a careful man. I believed firmly in the logarithm tables, the infallibility of the slide rules, and (to a lesser extent) the figures of the U. S. Census. But the graphs on my office wall seemed to be undulating with a gentle wave motion, and far below Lexington Avenue was developing a definite wriggle, like a happy snake.

I tried to keep my voice steady. "Miss Maddox," I said, "can you drink a glass of water without getting your mouth wet?"

"Why, no," she said, looking at me suspiciously. "Can you?"

"No," I said, "but I can't add up a column of figures, either, without having the figures first. Can you?"

'I'm not at all good at arithmetic. I majored in abnormal psychology-" She stopped abruptly there, but it seemed to me that she would have liked to say, "and I'm a little worried about you."

"Then how in the world did you get the final results without getting the individual results first?"

"I've always did it that way. I just filled in those papers afterward so it would come out right. I'll do it again if you like, but that's the hardest part, and it does seem silly to me."

I don't remember what I said to that, but I do recall asking her to try to stay within reach of our office. And as she went out, I noticed that she had very pretty legs. It also struck me suddenly that ever since I'd seen her the day before, I hadn't once thought of asking Diana for a date.

Miss Maddox was followed almost immediately by the man from Clark Investigating. He had come with her, so to speak.

"You look pretty tired," I said.

"That's right."

"Did you follow her all night?"

"No, I'm on the day shift. I'm just a little washed out from yesterday."

"Did you stay on her trail?"

"I didn't lose her, mister. I got it all here, with the time sequence."

I skimmed down the list and saw bar, bar, bar, bus, subway, hire boat. I jumped.
"Hire boat?"

"That was on City Island, mister. Oh, we been around."

"Maybe you'd better just tell me."

"Well, in a nutshell, we start off easy. She goes into a booth downstairs and makes a phone call. No answer. See, I'm in the next booth. She calls again. This time, I get a pretty good idea of the numbers from the clicks on the dial. That Havemeyer number is there. Still no answer. So she walks to Fifty-third Street, and we go down the subway and get an E train to Jackson Heights. Then we walk to an old sort of beat-up apartment house, and she goes in. Down by the door, she rings the bell."

"Whose bell?"

"Mister, I'm tailin' her, I ain't riding piggyback. Nobody answers, so she runs along, and I mosey up and copy down the names — eight of 'em — you got 'em there. Then's when we hit the bars. You ever been in Jackson Heights, mister?"

"Once or twice."

"Well, out there the bars are spread out, so we walk. Maybe two blocks between bars, mostly under the elevated. But no drinks! She just hits the bar long enough to ask if the guy is there."

"Who?"

"MacInnes. It's down on the paper."

"MacInnes?" It was the first time I'd heard his name. "MacInnes. I pick up the drift of what she's doin', so I beat her to the third bar. I'm standin' there with a fresh beer when she comes in, sort of easy like she wasn't used to floating into bars. She goes right straight up to the barkeep-see, it's early, and the bar's pretty empty-and says, 'Do you know Mr. MacInnes?' And the guy says, 'Old Mac?' 'Yes,' she says, and the guy says he ain't been to this bar for a couple of days, and maybe he's somewhere else down Roosevelt Avenue, and maybe he's fishin'.

"So we go moseyin' along horn bar to bar, and pretty soon I figure she thinks the guy has gone fishin'. Back we go on the E train to Manhattan, then we grab the Lexington Avenue clear up to Pelham Bay Park, end of the line. Then we hope a bus out to City Island, and she gets out at a boat yard. You know, City Island, mostly boat yards, and this time of year it looks like a cemetery. Nobody around, only a few schmoes working on boats hauled up onto the land."

"Did she find Macinnes?"

"She looks out on the water and there's only this rowboat. She hollers at the boat. 'Uncle Mac!' she hollers like that. No dice. The old bugger is just setting there. So she scrounges around the boat yard and gets a guy to hire her a boat."

"It says here that you hired a boat."

"Yeah. After she shoves off, I get to thinking, this is a hell of a place to try to tail somebody. So I try to rustle me up a boat, too. And with one eye, I'm keeping a lookout on what gives with the dame and the old guy."

"What did they do?" I suppose I was sitting forward in my chair, looking bug-eyed.

"I don't get it. This Maddox dame brings a stack of papers out there in the boat, and shows 'em to the old guy. He stops fishin', and for a hell of a long time, maybe twenty minutes, he just sits there lookin' at the papers. I had it figured for maybe process-servin' or maybe makin' a horse book or even the numbers-but twenty minutes! It don't fit. Well, I just finished paying the boat-yard guy to rent me his own boat, and I see they're comin' back, both of 'em."

"What about the papers now?"

"I guess the business is all over. She's got 'em packed away."

"Did they look like this?" I said, showing him the papers that Miss Maddox had just brought in.

"Could be, sure. Well, I see it's too late to go boatin', so I figure I'll just have to tail her back home. But what happens? This guy MacInnes — it's MacInnes, all right, I asked the guy at the boat yard — he's got a car. It's really beat up, like the guy lived in it. Maybe ten years old, paint job almost all wore off, and an old sweater wrapped around the front of it."

"Well, I make myself scarce when they come by, and they get into the jalopy. The old guy rolls himself a cigarette, lights up, and off they go, leavin' me standin' there, and maybe not a cab on the whole of City Island."

"You lost her there?"

"Jeez, yes. I climb back on the bus and the subway, and when I get back to town, I call up the dame. You know, the routine is you get the wrong number. She's home. I give the old guy time to get back to Jackson Heights, and I call him up, too. He's home."

"Did she go out again?"

"Yeah. To the movies. With her girlfriend."

I felt a whole lot better. Didn't seem to be much doubt that the one I was after was Macinnes. "What does this Macinnes look like?" I asked.

"Funny-lookin' old duffer. Must be sixty-five, seventy. Skinny, with kind of a hooked nose. Had a sweater wrapped around his neck like a muffler and the rattiest old suit you ever saw."

"Maybe that was just because he was fishing."

"Could be."

"Did you put down his address?"

"Address, phone number, license number, names and addresses of six bars where they know him, and the name of the boat yard. All down there."

A few minutes after that, Clark Investigating was gone, and I was sitting there, smiling an evil smile, and clutching in my two hands the address, phone number, and fraternal affiliations of Victor V. MacInnes.

PULP CULTURE PRESS

CHAPTER THREE

I didn't have any trouble recognizing him. He was in the fourth bar I tried along Roosevelt Avenue in Jackson Heights, sitting on a stool right in front of the television set. A wrestling match was on the screen, and MacInnes was looking at it and laughing. He wasn't drunk. He wasn't even high. He had a beer in front of him, and even though it was only down about a third of the way, it had a stagnant look, with the head gone, and the bubbles pretty tired. One of the wrestlers made a big squirm to bring his face into the camera and then gave out with a combination groan, snarl, and a look that said, "See, no hands!"

MacInnes laughed. He was tall and skinny and sort of bent over, but apparently from choice and not from infirmities. He wore the pants to an old blue suit, the coat to an old brown one, and under the coat an old raveled gray sweater that buttoned up the front. His shirt looked clean but shapeless, as though he'd washed it out himself in the washbowl and hadn't bothered to iron it. I sat on the stool next to him and ordered a beer. Then I dragged out a bag of tobacco and some cigarette papers and started to roll a cigarette. Hadn't done it since I was a kid, so I was making a mess.

Macinnes looked over at me. "You spit on it too much, sonny. You tryin' to put the fire out?"

"Guess I'm not very good at it," I said. "Haven't been doing it long. Thought I'd cut down on the price of smokes."

"Do it myself. I like the handmade ones better. Watch this, sonny." He pulled out his own tobacco, rolled a cigarette with one hand, and lit it with a great flare-up of paper. "Set myself on fire twice," he said, turning back to the television.

I rolled another one, with less spit, and lit it. "Mmmmmm. Better," he said. "Good smoke, huh?"

"Great," I said. It tasted like burning sycamore leaves. The commercial came on in the television, and MacInnes looked away. "I wonder if you'd help me," I said. "I've only got one more of these damned things to do before I go home. You just have to answer a few of these questions."

"More questions, sonny?"

"Did somebody else ask you some?"

"Skip it, boy, skip it. What's your problem?"
I hauled out four tubes of shaving cream-no labels, just the shiny metal, and with numbers one, two, three, four on them. I squeezed out a little of each one.

SEX MACHINE

Light green, white, pink, and cream color.

"Which color do you like?" I said.

"Mighty pretty. They're all nice."

"But which one do you like?"

"Which one do you like, son?"

"Well, I like the-" I stopped. "Look, it doesn't matter what I like!"

"Why not? Don't gulp that beer, son. Put it down easy."

"Yeah. Sure. I mean, they don't care what I like. I'm trying to get opinions. Survey, you know."

"Forget about that. You pick out the one you like."

I was beginning to get that lightheaded feeling again, and the one beer didn't have a thing to do with it. "Maybe you don't understand," I said. "We're trying to find out what color the public favors."

"The hell with the public. Now, I don't mean that unkindly, sonny. I mean, what business you got makin' an average color that everybody ought to like and havin' a machine turn out a hundred million of 'em? You trying to make everybody use the same color toothpaste?"

"Shaving cream.

"Are you?"

"Well, I-"

"You like the color of this tie?" It had a moldy color, like something that has been sitting around in a damp climate.

"Well—" I said.
"Say it, boy! You don't like it! Fine! *I* do! Now wouldn't it be awful if everybody had the same color tie?"

"I guess so. Maybe I'd better have another beer."

"Just don't gulp it, sonny."

"All right." I drank a little of it slowly, trying to keep my hand steady. "See, I'm just working for a salary. I ask questions. It's a living. I've got to get the answers to all the questions on all sixty of these papers before tomorrow night."

"Fellow said rain tomorrow. Right here on the television, a half-hour ago."

"Guess I'll get wet."

"Just to get down answers to those little questions?"

"Uh-huh."

"Then start askin', sonny."

"Which color?"

"Don't like any of 'em. How about a yellow beer color? Might be cheerful in the morning."

"It's got to be one of these."

"Yeah. Say this one. White. Matter of fact, they'd probably like white."

"Who would?"

"No," he said. "No. Not white. Cream color. That one. They'd like the cream color."

"Who would?"

"Hell, sonny, how do I know? Folks you're makin' it for, I guess."

"We were thinking primarily of urban males between the ages of eighteen and seventy."

"I was just thinkin' about shavin' cream. You don't figure you'd get much of a rise out of women on that, do you?"

"I don't know." I figured this was the pay dirt all right. "What about second place?"

"The white."

"Are you sure?"

"Nothin's sure, sonny."

"Third?"

"That's close. Let me see that green color again, sonny."

"There." He looked at it a moment.

"That's it, all right. Make it number three."

So I had the preferences ranked, in order: one, two, three, four. But Maddox's predictions had been fairly accurate even to the percentages. "You couldn't translate those choices into percentages, could you?"

"Percentages of what?"

"Of all the people. I mean, like sixty percent like the cream color, thirty percent the white, and so on."

"You figure I'm some kind of lightning calculator? Some kind of a crackpot, sonny?"

"Of course not."

"Watch the fight, boy. That's quite an act the fellow with the beard is putting on."

I looked. The wrestlers were at it again. We looked at them without saying anything until the bout was over.

"Listen," I said. "About those percentages-"

"You sure got a one-track mind, sonny."

"Maybe it'll be raining tomorrow. If I had some figures, I could sit home and maybe fake these surveys."

"Wish I could help you. Never had any head for figures."

"You think half the people would like the cream color?"

"Nope. Pretty near as many would like the white. Other two, the green and the pink are about the same, too, but only half as much as the first two. But I don't understand percentages."

"Just get a pencil for about two minutes. You can figure it, even without a slide rule. It works out this way."

Cream color - About 35 %
White   -About 32%
Green   -About 18%
Pink -About 15%
Total 100%

Change any one of those numbers more than about two percent and you'll find it won't work out the way MacInnes said. I tried it. But I didn't have time to do any paperwork right there in the bar.

"How do you know?" I asked. (Remember me, I'm the fellow with the slide rule and those big pieces of graph paper with the little squares and the lines. A week before, I wouldn't have been caught dead in a bar in Jackson Heights, exploring
the mental nip-ups of an old duffer warming up a glass of stale beer.) "I mean," I went on, "how can you tell that the adult urban male population of the United States likes cream colored soap for shaving?"

"Guess nobody could do that."

"You just did."

"I just said folks would like it."

"How do you know?"
"You ever walk into a room, sonny, and know right away the people didn't like you?"

"Uh-huh."

"They say something to you, cuss at you, or the like of that?"

"No."

"They frown at you; they look tough?"

"No."

"Then how'd you tell?"

I had to think for a minute on that one, but it didn't help much. "I don't know. You just feel it."

"How long's it take to feel it?"

"It doesn't take time. I mean, you either feel it or you don't. Right away."

"You suppose everybody feels it?"

"I don't know," I said. "Some people are supposed to be more sensitive than others."

"You're gettin' warm, sonny."

"Oh, no," I said. "You can't be that sensitive!"

"Didn't ask to be. Don't want to be. No good in it, boy."

"Maybe there could be."

"Hmmmmm?"

"I mean, maybe there could be something in it for you."

"Forget it, sonny."

"I won't forget it. Let me take down your name and address." I had them both, but I had to make it look real. He gave them to me. "But don't fool your-self, boy," he said. "Long as I can remember, I been the most sensitive man in the whole U. S. A., and it ain't worth a cent." He started to laugh again, but it wasn't at me. The intermission was over, and the wrestlers were going to it.

So I sat there, watching a couple of clowns push and grunt and mug at the camera and wondering whether the seedy-looking Scotsman at my side was really the most sensitive man in the United States. Or maybe in the whole histo-ry of the world. And if he was, what was I going to do about it?

"You mean," Colt said, "he just sat there at the bar and called off the an-swers?"

"That's right." It was almost two o'clock in the morning, but we were still awake, lying on our box-spring-and-a-mat tress beds, looking at the ceiling. I'd told Colt the whole thing because I had to tell somebody."

"And he was on the beam?"

"Perfect."

"He might have read your mind."

"No, he couldn't have. I had the figures in my pocket but didn't know them. I was thinking he might be psychic that way."

"Holy mackerel," said Colt softly. "It's a million dollars. It must be at least a million."

"That's what I thought too, at first," I said. "Why not now?"

"It won't work. Suppose Macinnes is perfect and stays that way. It won't make any difference."

"Why not?"

"In our business, you never sell results, you sell your method. How you made the survey, how many people you talked to, how many questions were asked, dozens of breakdowns of figures. Sometimes it takes a hundred pages."

"What if you skip all that?" Colt asked.
"You can't. The first person to see your report is usually another character like me, with a slide rule."

"Oh, you'd give 'em all that."

"How?"

"Haven't you any, imagination, Beech?" Not very much. "What difference would it make if you faked all that method business if you could give 'em the right results at a third the price?"

"You couldn't do that."

"This Maddox girl fooled you for a long time. And she was pretty crude."

"It's unsound and dishonest. I wouldn't do it."

"Let's put it this way. What does the poll system mean to you?"

"It's a living." I rolled over. "Let's go to sleep."

"It's more than that to you," Colt said, wide awake andl punching away. "One time, you told me what this whole business meant to you. It was very inspiring."

"You didn't seem to be inspired at the time."

"I couldn't see the buck in it. Now I'm inspired. I'm glow ing. You said the day would come when the polls would reach perfection, and on that day, we'd have a form of pure democracy, kind of a nationwide town meeting. Through the polls, the people would make clear their will."

"Uhmmmmmh," I said. He was so irradiated with Pure Democracy I could almost see him glow in the dark. "Go to sleep."

"You sounded so sincere when you said it."

"I felt sincere. Now I feel sleepy." I admit it now. I did believe all those things. Once that all the polls needed was greater accuracy, greater scope. With that achieved we might one day (I believed then) enter a kind of Hooper Gallop uto-pia, a Super-Jeffersonian promised land, dedicated to satisfying automatically the will of the majority.

Remember that was before MacInnes.

"What's stopping us?" asked Colt. "Suppose MacInnes has achieved perfection?"

"It wouldn't matter. No company would believe you for long without checking your method."

"Here's a switch. You don't have a method."

"What do you tell people?"

"The truth. You tell them about MacInnes."

"They wouldn't believe it."

"You can make people believe anything," said Beech, "if you sell 'em right."

"No," I said, "I think you're wrong. You'd be trying to get people to believe in something mental, and you'll never get Americans to do that. Make it technical, make it electronic, do it with a gadget, and they'll believe anything. Tell them you're getting steam heat from the moon by radar, and they'll swallow it without a murmur, but tell them you can throw a single thought twelve inches, and they'll call you a liar."

"Mmmmmm," said Colt.

"What?" I asked.

"I was just thinking," he said. And so he was, but I didn't realize what a monstrous bee I'd put in his bonnet as I dropped off to sleep. And then, like a nuclear explosion, it hit me. MacInnes was wrong. Dead wrong, right there on paper. I'd given Miss Maddox two surveys, one of them on the selection of colors for automobiles. Several days later, our own results started to come in. Temple sent for me.

"Fire that Maddox girl," he said.

"But the detective proved," I said, "that it isn't a ring. He said that-" I don't know. My ears seemed to be ringing with that soft, slightly Southern accent, and I felt I had to defend her. But without mentioning MacInnes. That was my secret.

"She had a run of luck," Temple said. "Coincidence. Hunches. I've seen other fakers do it. But she's two miles off on this auto colors job. The Eastern states are almost complete, and she isn't even close."

I started to open my mouth, but the figures were right there in front of me.

MacInnes was wrong.

"Fire her," said Temple. "And forget the whole thing."

I looked across the red-checkered tablecloth at Miss M. L. Maddox.

"Do you always fire people like this, Mr. Beecher?" She was wearing a knitted blouse that brought out the worst in me, and smiling pleasantly.

"My name," I said, "isn't Mr. Beecher. It's-it's Fred.

" I don't care how you say that, it always sounds silly. "Fred-Peggy. It will save a lot of time," she said. We were in a "little" French restaurant on Third Avenue. "Little" means you can get lunch for about a buck. Another French restaurant nearby will cost you three or four. Though it is exactly the same size, it is never referred to as "little."
"I just thought," I said, "that a bouillabaisse might soften the blow. That is if you like bouillabaisse."

"I always get sort of tangled up in it. What's this?" I looked at the menu. It was one of those purple hecto graphed jobs, handwritten in a wobbly French script. My four years of French didn't make a dent in it.

"What's this?" I asked the waiter.

"Mussels."

"And what's this?"

"Mussels, monsieur."

"What's the difference?"

"Is steamed. Is baked."

"Oh, look!" I said. "Filet of sole au vin blanc." That I could read. We settled for the sole and a small pitcher of sauterne. "May I borrow your sugar?" asked a large, steely-eyed man whose table was one and a half inches away from ours.

"Of course," I replied. It was very intimate. On the other side, also one and a half inches away, were two plump women who were talking about innerspring mattresses.

"It was awfully nice of you," said Peggy, "to see about that other job." I'd talked to a friend of mine at another research outfit where I used to work. He said he'd give Peggy a try.

"But, remember," I said, "this time, you've really got to make the surveys.

SEX MACHINE

Honestly. Just going and asking your uncle is like stuffing the ballot box, it's like-"

"What did you say?"

I knew I'd slipped there. "Hmmmmm?" I asked innocently.

"How did you know my uncle had anything to do with this?"

"Does he?"

"How do you even know I have an uncle,"

"We made a survey. Practically everybody has an uncle. They're thinking about declaring Uncle's Day."

"You know about my Uncle Mac." I just kept quiet. "Not only that," she said, "but I believe you talked to him the other night. He said that a young man with a short haircut
and horn-rimmed spectacles talked to him in a bar in Jackson Heights. He had some surveys, and he asked a lot of questions."

I still didn't say anything.

"How did you find out he was my uncle?"

"Really, Peggy-"

"I remember now. That day you called me in for a special job. There was a big man in a blue shirt, and I could swear he followed me all the way out to City Island. Why—you you were having me tailed!" She tried to stand up, but she was sitting on one of those benches against the wall and the table in front of her. You can't be indignant in a spot like that.

"All right, all right," I said.

The two ladies stopped talking about mattresses. They and the steely-eyed man on the other side were staring at us.

"You admit it!"

"I just thought," I said, "that history would forgive me."

"Well, I won't."

"You don't realize what I thought. I thought you really had some miraculous way of reaching into the minds of a hundred million people. Do you know what that would mean to the world?"

"Do you?" Now that she was angry, her Southern accent was in full bloom.

"Yes!" I was shouting, too. And more Midwestern probably. "All it means is utopia, that's all. It means that the will of the people will be registered, like temperature."

"Is that good?"

"It's perfect!" (I'm just putting this down the way I said it, remember. I believed it all then that was before the real MacInnes Episode.) "You see," I went on, "all Western civilization has been heading for this. It's the ultimate development of democracy. The system of voting has become too cumbersome."

"But sometimes more accurate."

"We're changing that. I even hoped your uncle might change it overnight. See, our society is too big, too complex. You can't have forums and town meetings anymore. A real way to register opinion immediately would mean a paradise on earth." Yes, I really believed it, then. "I might have known it couldn't come true so quickly."

"What couldn't come true?"

"MacInnes. I really thought he had that power.

She looked at me very strangely, the way, I suppose, people looked at Robert Fulton or Alexander Graham Bell before the movies made them famous. I hoped she thought I was brilliant, yes, but unstable, slightly mad.

"Do you feel all right, Fred?"

"Mmmmmm?"

"We had a little dog once. He got that same look in his eyes, and he went out and bit somebody." We were all pilloried, we were all spat upon. Fulton, Eli Whitney, the Wright brothers, all of us.

"All I meant was that we might have passed into the Golden Age if your uncle, Mr.
MacInnes, could do what I thought he could do."

"Oh, you mean if he could always give the right answers on those mimeographed papers you send me."

"That's all. Just make light with electricity. Just make steam move a wheel. Why, if your uncle could really answer every one of those questions correctly, he'd be the new savior of mankind. The new Messiah."

"I don't believe it."

"It's true."

"Well, he can. There isn't any doubt at all that he can, and you know as well as I do that nothing has ever happened because of it. Except that, I turned in some very good answers that you never appreciated at all."

"Believe me, I once thought he could do it, too. It would have changed the whole course of history. And, of course, it would have made him one of the wealthiest and most famous men in the world."

"Then," said Peggy, 'Tm certainly glad you think he can't do it. Don't you ever try to make Uncle Mac wealthy and famous."

"Why not?"

"Because I think he's the only completely happy man in the whole world. Wasn't always that way, either. Mother used to tell me about him. She was his sister. He worked for a bank in a little town near Baltimore. You know, stiff collar, shoe always shined, always at work at eight-thirty on the dot, always caring what 'people' might think about anything he did. He had a beautiful wife, too, Mother said. I never saw her. She ran away with an artist before I was born. She left him a copy of Thoreau and a railroad timetable. He never was exactly sure what she meant, but he quit the bank, and he stopped caring what people thought about anything. Well, he got over it, and now I suppose he's the most independent man in the whole world. And you'd better not change him, Fred Beecher, or you'll hear from me."

"Don't worry," I said. "The episode is over. MacInnes is safe. And the world is back again in the darkness." The waiter came with our fish and the pitcher of sauterne. The steely-eyed man stood up, and the two plump ladies resumed their discussion of innerspring mattresses.

That evening if you'd seen me on the Lexington Avenue bus, you might have thought, "Who's the little guy with the portable slide rule and the rosy expression?" I had a date with Peggy Maddox for Saturday night. Nothing, I thought, as I sauntered into our apartment, could dismay me.

"Y-ipe!" I said as I opened the door.

''Step in, professor," said Colt.

I did. I just stood still, with a glazed look. Our living room was filled, to half its cubic capacity, with the damnedest mess of machinery you ever saw. It was as big as a Cadillac, but it didn't look like a Cadillac. Just imagine the inside of a radio, the tubes, the wires, and the coils. Multiply that by about a hundred, and add in the works of the vacuum cleaner, the washing machine, the oil burner, and the hot water heater. Press them all haphazardly into a pile about nine feet high, and you've got a picture of what I saw.

"And it's all ours," said Colt.

"What is it?"

"I don't know. I haven't named it yet."

''Oooooh.''

"I thought you'd like it." He stood there, his fat rosy face beaming paternally.

"Where did you get it?"

"The War Assets people let me have it. The fellow said it cost the govern-ment twenty-three thousand bucks. He let me have it for $128.37. Isn't that a bargain?"

"Where did you get the hundred and twenty-eight bucks?"

"My allowance came this morning. And I had to hock your typewriter. Isn't room for it anymore, anyway."

"There isn't room for us, either. What does it do?"

"It's got something to do with controlling the firepower of a battleship."

"Does it work?"

"Not very well, I guess, without the battleship. As a matter of fact, he said they didn't think very much of this model. Never used it, because a new one came out."

"Then what good is it?" In the back of my head, I was thinking of the conver-sation we'd had the other night, but I wanted to hear him say it himself.

"It's perfect. It has seventy-four dials, and it lights up in twenty-three differ-ent places. Nobody could understand it, not even a man with a slide rule."

"I should have kept my mouth shut."

"No, you were right, Beech. What you said to me that night about gadgets and machinery, well, it was an inspiration. I stayed awake most of the night, and the next day I went out looking for a whoozie, anything with an engineering degree. And let me tell you, the War Assets is a gold mine."

"I'll bet."

"I could have got some bigger stuff, but we'd have had to move into the kitchen."

" Is this big, enough?"

"I think so."

"You can't send it back?"

"Who wants to send it back? Beech, don't start being cynincal and defeatist now. Just picture this. We make a deal with Macinnes. We do a terrific selling job. Here's the greatest invention since Hooper ratings. It's a machine for measuring public opinion. Know how the lie detector works? Electricity!"

"Look, Colt—" I started.

"That's how this works, on a gigantic scale. It's electronic. You invented it, we say."

"Colt, listen—"

"You don't understand it yourself. It's like radar. It picks up brain waves. Look into that tube, and you've got your hand on the pulse of the nation."

"Which tube?"

"Any tube. Wait'!! I get somebody to hook it up. It looks like a pinball machine giving birth to its young. What's the reaction of the trade? They think we're a couple of screwballs. We offer the service to some guys free. 'Don't believe it,' we say. 'Just write down the answers, and in a couple of weeks, when the old-style surveys come in, compare the results.'"

"That's what I'm trying to point out," I said. "It's all off. I don't believe in Macinnes anymore." It was like telling a child there isn't any such thing as Santa Claus or Bing Crosby. I thought for a minute he was going to cry. Then I told him what had happened at the office.

"I don't believe it," he said. "It was a coincidence."

"The others must have been coincidences. He's uncanny, sure, but it's a trick, like reading tea leaves. You can't start a business on that basis."

"Why didn't you tell me," he wailed, "before I bought this Erector set?"

"I just heard about it today." So we stood there, looking at our furniture, which barricaded one side of the living room, and at the Gimmick, which sat there quietly, staring back at us.

It may have been my imagination, but it seemed to me that the gadget had a smug and superior look, as though its dials were just perceptibly raising their eyebrows. But then you'd probably strut a bit if you knew you could sink a battleship twenty miles away in very unpleasant weather.

CHAPTER FOUR

And then we discovered that MacInnes had never been wrong at all. The next day I found out that when Diana brought me the final results of the survey on auto colors, the one we thought MacInnes had missed by a mile. "This'll throw you," she said, sashaying out with a healthy swaying of the shoulders and a vigorous but pure wriggling of the hips. (At this point, I told myself my interest in Diana was purely clinical.)

The new auto-colors results were mainly from the West, and as I went through them, I remembered that cars from out there, especially California, wore less inhibited colors. Business coupes were often beige, orchid, and shocking pink — and, generally, other colors used in the East for snoods, sandwich fillings, and tea-shop curtains.

I pulled out MacInnes' answers and was shocked to see that these eccentric tastes pulled the national averages right over to Mac's figures. On the button. Think about that for a minute. There was MacInnes, sitting in a rowboat in the middle of Eastchester Bay. Somehow, a technicolor brain wave came into his skinny old head, telling him that ten thousand Californians liked peach-colored convertibles. And yet, you may say, if he'd had a portable radio the size of a camera, no one would have considered it miraculous for him to listen to the short wave from London.

I phoned Colt. "I'll call you back," he said. "I've got a junk man here. He says there may be twenty dollars worth of copper wire in this thing, and who knows what else?"

"Don't sell it yet. Wait till I talk to you."

"Look," he said, "we've had chile con carne for three nights in a row."

"Maybe he could just pull out five, ten dollars' worth of wire now. We'll never miss it."

"I'll ask him.,." I heard him ask something.

"No," Colt said, "he's gotta take it all or nothing. Tell me, Beech, have you got something new on Macinnes?"

"I can't talk now," I said. Hang onto the gadget. I'll try to get home early." As I put down the phone, I thought of Temple and what his reaction might be if he saw the new figures on auto colors side by side with the Macinnes results. I took the Maddox-Macinnes surveys, tore them up, and dropped them into my waste-basket. "Let Temple ask me," I thought. I could tell him I'd fired the girl and destroyed her results. And there, as far as Standard-Idea Research was concerned, the incident was closed.

But for Colter Fleming and Fred Beecher, it had scarcely begun. That night, we had frankfurters and beans served with mustard and dreams of glory. I cooked the solid food, and (according to our custom) Colt took care of the nourishment for our spirits.

"What'll you have?" he said. "Wealth? Power? Beautiful girls?"

"I'd like to get that battleship out of the living room."

"That'll be sooner than you think. We'll get a suite of offices. Who knows, maybe after a year or so, we'll put up our own building."

"First, maybe we ought to call Macinnes and find out if he wants to be part of your rosy dream."

"Okay. You call him tonight."

"I'll find out when it would be convenient for him to have us come out there and see him."

"No," Colt said, "find out when he can come here."

"Why?"

"We're going to have to put on an act and the Gimmick there is going to be one of the props."

Well, Macinnes made it. It took us two nights to reach him, and then he didn't want to come. "You got a television set?" he asked over the phone.

"I don't think so," I said.

"What do you mean, you don't think so? You got one or you haven't got one, sonny."

"We've got kind of a combination here. Maybe there's television. We just haven't found it yet."

"You call me when you find it, sonny. They got the boxing tonight."

"How about tomorrow?"

"I'll look at the paper." He went away from the phone, and he must have been gone for ten minutes. "Here it is," he said. "Couldn't find it right off. Always save the Sunday Times. Got the schedule for the whole week. No. No wrestling, no boxing. Not a damn thing but a couple of drama shows."

"You'll make it, then? Give you all the beer you can drink."

"Never did like drama shows. You feel the same way, sonny?"

"I don't mind 'em," I said.

"Sure," he said, "you can't hear the guy gruntin' m the background."

"Gruntin'?"

"Yep. Me, I can always hear the guy gruntin' backstage. Maybe it's the fellow who wrote it, maybe somebody else. I can just feel the way he was pushin' it around, puttin' in angles to pull in the audience, gruntin' like hell to make sure folks would like it. That's the same reason I had to quit going to the movies. I always heard the guy gruntin' back there."

I didn't quite get his point then, but I didn't care. "You mean you'll come tomorrow night?"

"Try to, sonny."

So, as I say, Macinnes made it. The next evening, he drove his car over the Queensboro Bridge from Jackson Heights and rang our doorbell at about nine o'clock. It wasn't cold, but he came in wearing an overcoat with a big but mangy old fur collar.
"Keep warm, I always say, sonny; keep warm, and you'll live longer." Underneath, he had on the same old suit and sweater he was wearing that night in the bar. I introduced him to Colt, who was fiddling with the Gimmick.

"Think I've finally got it working," Colt said, wiping his forehead, just as though he'd really done it himself. He'd had a radio repair man fooling around with it all afternoon, putting in a transformer and fixing it so some of the tubes and dials would light up.

"That the television set, sonny?" Mac said.

Colt just kept looking at Mac, and MacInnes kept looking at the Gadget. I don't know which one looked queerer, the Gadget to MacInnes or Macinnes to Colt.
"This," said Colt, "is the most amazing invention of the ages."

"Got a nice big screen," said Mac. "Too bad there's no wrestling on tonight."

"It isn't television," said Colt flatly. "It's a Psychoelectronic Correlator."

"The only one of its kind," I said, "in the whole world." We were positive of it. We made up the name ourselves.

SEX MACHINE

"That so?" said MacInnes, getting out his tobacco and rolling a cigarette. He was sitting in one of our two easy chairs, sitting forward so that his head hung down like a buzzard on a dead tree. He'd had a good look at the machine, and now he was ready to forget it.

"Know how much it's worth?" said Colt. "Forty-eight thousand dollars!"

That made MacInnes more interested.

"He invented it," Colt said, looking at me.

"Not entirely," I said modestly. "I combined some mighty ingenious devices developed during the war. Anyone might have stumbled into it."

"What's it good for?" Mac asked.

Colt said, "It's a multiple co-ordinator of brain impulses. Though I don't expect you to believe it right away."

"I think Mr. MacInnes has more mental equipment to believe it than anyone else," I said. "That's why I asked him to come in town tonight." Macinnes shot me a look over his sputtering homemade cigarette, and I knew I wasn't fooling him with any of that kind of soft soap.

"What's it good for?" Mac repeated.

"It registers automatically what people are thinking. Over the whole country."

"What's the matter with you boys?" Mac asked. "You got no minds of your own, payin' all that money to find out what some other fellows eight states away are thinking? Seems to me like an awful waste of hardware."

"Ought to pay for itself in a year," Colt said. "Maybe six months."

"Forty-eight thousand dollars?"

"Maybe more," Colt added.

"Where's that money coming from?"

"Well," I said, "from all kinds of people. From a man who has a radio program, or an advertising campaign in a magazine, or a factory that makes anything sold to the public. Or the people who make movies, or publish books, or magazines. Politicians, too."

"They'd pay all that money just to find what people are thinking?"

"They're paying fifty times that now," said Colt, "just to find out what people were thinking two, three weeks ago. Figure out some way to find what they're thinking now, and you've got a million."

MacInnes sat there for a minute, just blinking. "Looks to me," he said, "like I've been wastin' a lot of time."

"You'll make up for it." I turned to Colt. "Is the machine warmed up?"

"Ready to go!" Colt replied/

"The only thing we need," I said, "is an operator. We were wondering if you'd be interested, Mr. MacInnes."

"Not me, sonny. Don't know a thing about machinery."

"You don't have to," I said.

"All you have to do," said Colt, "is slide this little piece of metal." Colt slid the piece of metal, which was just a simple rheostat we'd had the radio man hook up on the circuit. When you pushed it back and forth, it made the lights go up and down. We also had a stylus arrangement hooked up to it, to record where the rheostat had been.

"You see," I said, "it isn't just a matter of pushing a piece of metal. You have to know where to push it. You have to be in tune with public opinion."

"Sit right here," said Colt.
MacInnes sat and put his hand gingerly on the rheostat. "This is the range," I said. "This is zero, and this is a hundred percent. If half the people are in favor of something, you push the button out to here-fifty percent. See?"

"All I do is push it?"

"Uh-huh," said Colt. "Everything else is automatic."

"Let's try a test run," I said. "I've got a question here. How many men like to sleep with just their pajama tops on?"

"I don't know," said MacInnes. "All these wires get me kind of mixed up."

"Maybe," said Colt, "we could fix up some kind of blinders."

"Just look at the little button," I said, "and think about pajama tops."

"I'm tryin', sonny. Nothin' seems to be comin' through."

"Maybe," Colt said, "all the men in the U. S. aren't thinking about pajama tops."

I said "Shhhhh."

"Would it help," Colt asked, "if I went out and put on my pajamas?"

"How about a nice bottle of beer, Mr. MacInnes? Might help you to relax."

"Won't do any harm, sonny." I brought it, and he sat there, taking a few sips and watching the little bubbles rise. I reread the question and put my hand on the little button. I moved it. Some of the lights went on, some became brighter, some dimmer. One big tube sputtered. A red bulb went off, and a green one came on. It looked like Christmas in Macy's window. The rheostat was exactly halfway up.

"That much?" I said.

"Half of them?"

"Huh-uh. Not that many, sonny. More like about here." He slid the button back. It said thirty-one percent.

"Is it right?" Colt said.

"My sheet says twenty-nine percent, but my survey was taken two months ago. It was colder then."

MacInnes turned around and looked right at me. "You mean," he said, "you knew the answer all along?"

"I was just testing the machine. Works fine so far."

"Perfect," said Colt. "Did you see how the lights went up and down when Mr. MacInnes pushed the button?"

"Very convincing," I said.

MacInnes slid the button back and forth rapidly. The effect was similar to the aurora borealis. "Who you trying to convince?" he asked.

"The people who'll pay us the money," I said. "How about it? Would you like to go in with us?"

Macinnes sat at the machine, his finger on the button and a soggy old roll-your-own cigarette drooping unlit from his lips.

"I really believe," I said, "that we can do a real service to mankind."

"Don't you fool yourself, sonny. Folks won't thank you for handin' 'em their ideas back at 'em."

"I don't believe that," I said. "We'll be the interpreters of the voice of the people, and —" Colt jumped in. "You'll make more money than you ever saw before in your life."

Macinnes looked up. "Let's go on along those lines, boy," he said. "How much?"

"How about a flat ten percent of all our net profits?" said Colt.

"How do you figure net?" said Macinnes. "After whose salaries come out?"

I guess Colt thought he was going to deal with some kind of a swami with a head full of visions and a very fuzzy idea of cost accounting.
"Well —" said Colt. "'I had figured that we might deduct a reasonable salary for Mr. Beecher and myself."

"I think you're nice boys," Mac said. "I think you got a fine idea here. Maybe you ought to look around and see if you can find somebody else to run your machine."

"It has to be somebody who's very sensitive," I said.

"What you mean, sonny, is that this mess of wires and doodads is to bamboozle some unsuspectin' character who's got a hatful of simoleons. I've been wrong before, sonny, but the way I figure, this contraption wouldn't tell you the time of day without MacInnes sittin' at the throttle."

"Now wait —" said Colt.

"Not that it isn't a mighty pretty piece of hardware." He stood up, the old rag of a cigarette still sticking to one lip.

"Your share," said Colt, "might come to as much as a hundred thousand dollars.·•

"That's a lot of money," said MacInnes, starting toward the coat closet.

"Let's admit it, Colt," I said. "We can't run this business without Mr. MacInnes."

"How about twenty percent?" said Colt
.
Macinnes opened the closet door and reached for his coat. "What do you want, Mr. Madnnes?" I said.

He turned. "Boys," he said, "I don't think I ought to take less than fifty percent."

"That's impossible!" said Colt.

"Who's to stop me from goin' into business myself, now that you point out the profits? I can get me a hunk of machinery if that'll help, but can you go out and get another MacInnes?"

We just stood there for maybe ten seconds. I knew perfectly well that we couldn't get another MacInnes, I knew that MacInnes knew it, and I was pretty sure that Colt knew it, too.

Mac closed the closet door without taking his coat. He walked over to one of the easy chairs, threw away his old butt, and hauled out the bag of tobacco. His head was bent over, but he looked out at us through the tops of his eyes, the way a fellow will do when he's used to looking up over reading glasses. His mouth was stretched out a little in a smile. It was as much of a smile as I ever saw on MacInnes. In all the time I knew him, he never did smile enough to show his teeth, and I'm not completely sure that he had teeth, except that I've seen him eat things that had to be chewed.

"Scared you, didn't I, boys?"

"We knew you were kidding, Mac," I said. It was the first time I'd called him Mac. He didn't seem to mind.

"I wasn't," he said. "Fifty percent would be about right. But why be a hog? If there's all the money in this you say there is, won't be much difference in what the government leaves me, whether it's fifty percent, or, say, thirty-three and a third."

"A third?" said.Colt.

"I mean a third before you boys take out any salary. I mean after expenses are paid, the three of us split up the money, three ways."

"Now wait a minute—" said Colt.

"Why not?" I put in. "Looks to me as though we'll either rake in so much it won't make any difference, or we won't make anything at all."

"Well —" Colt began.

"Okay," I said. "It's agreed. A three-way split."

Mac smiled. "Thank you, boys. Maybe you think I'm an old bastard. Maybe it's just the banker in me comin' out. You know I used to be a banker? Money's my weakness, boys. Maybe that's just because I found out a few greenbacks in the bank gives you more freedom than a shack in the woods like Mr. Thoreau's. And I know. I tried it awhile. Tell you about that sometime."

We got out some more beer. Everybody felt a lot easier.

"You don't figure," Mac asked, "that this business will take much time, do you, sonny?"

"It shouldn't," I said. "Probably not more than an hour or so a day."

"Good. Just don't want to be tied down. That's the bad thing, boys, gettin' tied down. You want to have time to have fun. I feel like workin', I work. I feel like goin' fishin', I fish." Mac told us about his business, a little real estate and insurance office in Jackson Heights. Upstairs. Didn't even keep a regular stenographer or regular office hours.

"Just handle deals for a few old customers. Don't make much money. Knew a lot of fellows that did. All dead. Don't know a one of 'em ever had time to get any fun out of it. Maybe I'll put in five, ten hours a week. Plenty. Just be sure your standard of livin's workin' for you, not the other way around."

After a while Mac left. "Yippeee!" said Colt.

"I thought you were mad."

"I was mad, but he's right. There ought to be enough for him, and for you, and for me."

"If there's anything for anybody."

"There'll be plenty for everybody, Beechie. And that's a promise."

The photograph of Joe Smetana, hack license number 4276, with his cap on, framed and individually lit, stared impartially at Peggy and me. Joe himself was sitting up front, swinging the cab off Fifty-ninth Street and into Central Park. "Once upon a time," said Peggy, "people sat in front of fireplaces. And above the mantel, in the flickering light, was a portrait of an ancestor."

I don't know why. When a girl thinks she's going to be kissed, she always talks. Even, I believe, when she wants to be kissed, though at this point I wasn't entirely sure about Peggy.

"And now," she went on, "our glowing hearth is the hack license of Joe Smetana."

"Yes, lady;" asked Joe, turning around. The picture didn't do him justice.

57

SEX MACHINE

"Around the park," I said, "around the park."

Through the trees we could see the lights along the whole cliffside of Central Park South. It was about midnight on Saturday, and we'd been to a play. Our first date.

"It is beautiful, though," Peggy said.

"Who, Joe?"

"Yes, mister?"

"Around the park, around the park."

"You ain't on the Pulaski Skyway, mister." But Joe's voice was warm, and I think maybe he, too, had been in love.

"I mean," said Peggy, "the lights over the trees, and —" She smelled sweet and perfumey, and her lips were soft and warm. At about Seventy-Second Street, she put her arm around me, too. Up near 110th Street, when we turned to go back, she pulled away. Just a little bit away. And she held my hand tightly.

"You'll find," she said, "that I'm a strong-willed woman."

"That's what worries me." And as we rolled south, alongside Central Park West, one other thing worried me. I hadn't yet told her about the deal we'd made with MacInnes.
"Peggy —" I began.
.

"Yes, Fred?" She was smiling so pleasantly, and I thought —or maybe I hoped—that I saw a very, very warm look in her eyes. "Beautiful," I said.

"Who, Joe?" But this time, Joe kept on looking straight ahead. We didn't care. We had the picture—hack license number 4276, with the cap on. Our first client dropped right into our hands. It happened nearly two weeks after we'd made our deal with Mac. Meantime, of course, Colt had become intimate with several dozen receptionists around town, most of them at advertising agencies. No luck.

"What do you suggest?" I asked. "Tell Mac the deal is off?"

"Hell, no," Colt said. "There are plenty of angles we haven't tried yet. Publicity. Make a couple of fantastic predictions that we know will come true. An election, maybe."

"Does it have to be an election?"

"We might try direct-mail advertising. Make up a folder with pictures of the gadget and samples of results. Might even run an ad in some trade journals."

"What would all that cost?"

"The publicity, nothing, if you're lucky. The others, maybe a couple of hundred apiece."

It was two days till payday, and I had $1.75 in my pocket. "Let's try the publicity," I said.
But as it worked out, we were just lucky. Our office always closed at five-fifteen, but, barring emergencies, it was considered a social error to work after five. During the last fifteen minutes, the girls cleared their desks, powdered their noses, chattered, ran back and forth to Johnny, brushed their hair, and put on their coats.

I was heading for the john myself, plowing a wake through all this chirping and preening and trying not to get tagged with a stray swipe of pancake makeup. Outside of Temple's office, I heard some loud and excited talking. As I passed the door, it opened, and a little man bounded out. He was short, bald, and wore an expensive suit cut along sharp, uninhibited Broadway-Hollywood lines. He seemed to be talking with Temple, but he was in constant movement, like a man shadow-boxing.

"Well, geez, baby," he said to Temple so fast that the words all ran together. You can either do it or you can't do it, right? And if you can't do it, let me find somebody who can, right?"

"I think that's about it, Mr. Bascomb," Temple said.

"No hard feelings, huh, baby?" The little man smiled sweetly with big white teeth.

"No, not at all," said Temple, standing up big and solid. The little fellow's words echoed against him like a yodel on a cliff.

"See you in church, baby," said Bascomb, dancing off toward the reception room.

"Come in, Beecher," Temple said.

I went into his office, and Temple sat down wearily. "You look sort of beat up," I said.
"I'm just tired in the head. Bascomb is a two-ounce jigger of straight adrenalin with a thyroid chaser. Maybe you have to be in his business. Bascomb Productions."

"I've heard of them."

"They're agents for talent, mostly radio, and they produce some radio and television shows. Now he's poll-happy. The Hoopers aren't enough."

"Does he want a special survey?"

"All he needs," said Temple, "is somebody to spit on his finger and tell which way the wind is blowing. He wanted us to test out recordings of five different masters of ceremony all over the country and for twenty-five hundred dollars."

"That's ridiculous," I said. Already, I was beginning to think of Macinnes and twenty-five hundred dollars.

"That's what I told him. We couldn't begin to give him that kind of coverage in that time — and certainly not for that money."

So help me, I hadn't meant to say anything more about MacInnes to Temple. He was our baby, and we didn't want anybody else moving in. But I did feel sorry for Temple, sitting there in his shirt sleeves with the drops of sweat on his brow, as though his big headful of brains was trying to get out by some kind of osmosis.

"Any chance that Bascomb will come back?" I said. "If I call him and tell him we can do the job, yes."

"You think he might skip a little scientific accuracy?"

"The little flutterhead doesn't know what scientific accuracy is."

"Then I wish you'd let me talk to him. I know one thing we can do for twenty-five hundred."

"What?"

"You remember Miss M. L. Maddox?"

"The girl who faked those surveys?"

"Well, they weren't entirely faked. It was a peculiar process."

"Was it?" he said. He didn't even look skeptical. He just looked tired.

"I really believe it's genuine."

"Once before, you said it was a ring. Sort of a spy ring."

"I was wrong. It's mental. A hundred percent mental."

"Beecher, are you sure your condition isn't mental?"

"I'm serious. With this process, we can give Bascomb exactly what he wants and do it for twenty-five hundred."

"I could do it myself for fifty cents. Tea leaves. Astrology. A man came to us once with a divining rod. He said he could use it either for locating wells or testing public opinion."

"Those are crackpots. They're—"

"Beecher, we're running a research organization here, not a fortune-telling parlor."

"Right," I said. No doubt my mouth was a thin, grim line. "And besides, I thought I told you to fire Maddox."

"I did."

"All right. Let's hear no more about it."

So I left, and it wasn't until long after Macinnes arrived that I told Colt what I'd done. But I wasn't sorry. I'd always have felt we were double-crossing Temple when we made our deal with Bascomb.

CHAPTER FIVE

At Ten-thirty the following day, Colt and I were sitting in the outside office of Bascomb Productions. Though it was on the thirty-second floor of one of the highest and newest buildings of Radio City, the anteroom was known in the trade as the Colonial Kitchen.

The whole room tried very hard to give the impression it had been whittled out with a jackknife. The floors and walls were hand-hewn and pegged, and the furniture was wooden, quaint, and genuine. The chairs were as comfortable as an English saddle. After ten minutes, you wanted to post up and down.

"I think," said Colt, "we should have worn our three-cornered hats."

The receptionist looked at Colt listlessly. She was sitting behind a very severe table, plain and authentically worm-holed. The table, that is, not the girl. There was absolutely nothing Colonial about her. She was tall and dark, and looked exactly like Hedy Lamarr. Sitting by the brick-and-timber fireplace, not functional, were several henna-haired ingenues who looked quite functional, and blondes of various shades were scattered around by the break front and the old settee.

There were males, too, actors with long glossy hair, rough tweed coats, brightly colored shirts, and resonant voices. There was one smallish, bespectacled, introverted-looking fellow I assumed was a script writer, and two women with noisy and precocious children. They were all looking for work with Bascomb Productions, and Bascomb Productions was apparently looking for anything that would turn a comparatively honest buck. Colt said they had "package" radio productions, sold as an entire unit to the advertising agencies; that they were getting into television productions, too, and that they had a profitable sideline as a talent agency, selling talent to radio, television, Broadway, and, rarely. to the movies.

"Just think," said Colt, "it all started out with just one soap opera. Bascomb stumbled onto an option on 'The Bodkin Family' maybe ten or twelve years ago."

"I think it's still in the top ten in the daytime, Hooper," I said.

"He probably clears fifteen hundred a week on it now, over production cost, plus his commission on the writers and the two main stars. He always hires his own people. Sort of works both ends against the middle."

The receptionist's phone rang. "Mr. Bascomb will see you now," she said, looking briefly at us, and then back at her nails. "Down the end of that hall."
On the way, we noticed that the small offices on either side of the corridor

were violently Colonial, too. Sitting in them were, we assumed, Bascomb's contact men, script writers, casting and production directors, and publicity people. Bascomb's secretary, a tall angular girl who must have been selected by Mrs. Bascomb, met us part way.

"Go right in, Mr. Beecher," she said.

It was a corner office, about the size of a polo field. Bascomb was at the far corner, flanked on both sides by windows. Along one wall was a huge double turntable for playing sixteen-inch transcriptions, combined with a speaker, one of those horizontal record changers that would play two hundred standard records, a television set with a projection screen three feet square, and an AM-FM radio-the entire ensemble apparently having been designed by Thomas Jefferson and built with his own hands.

"Come in, baby," said Bascomb, looking up for one second. Like "deer" and "sheep," "baby" was apparently both singular and plural.

Bascomb had a thick stack of papers in front of him, letters, memos, and scripts, and he looked at them one after another for about four seconds, made a little check in one corner, and put it on another pile, face down. It wasn't like Temple's preoccupation and Temple's startled look when you came in. You had the feeling that Bascomb hadn't begun to look at the stack until you walked in the door.

"Well, baby," he said, looking up at last, "I knew Temple would come around if I gave him a little time."

"But, Mr. Bascomb—" I started. The little interoffice speaker on his desk made a humming noise.

"Mr. Bascomb," it said, "I have Mr. Something on the wire."

"Put him on," Bascomb said. "Hello, baby. Yeah, I know it dropped two points in the Hooper, but did you see the Nielson? Only down four-tenths.... Yeah, tell him that. It's just the old seasonal slump.... Sure, baby, I know she's a hot singer, but she's already on for Chesterfields. She can't handle any more tobacco. Yeah, I'll look into it, baby."

He hung up the phone. "Mr. Bascomb, I—"

"Just a second, baby. Let me get this while it's hot." He flipped a key on his speaker. "Gorgeous!" he said. "Yes, Mr. Bascomb."

"Will you get Fox to come in here for a second?"

"He's in the studio, Mr. Bascomb."

"Yeah, yeah. Put a note on his desk, will you, to see me right after lunch?"

"Yes, Mr. Bascomb."

"And, gorgeous," he said, "that reminds me. Will you check Laughlin over at NBC, and find out what about getting 6B for that audition on Tuesday?"

"Yes, Mr. Bascomb."

He took his hand off the speaker key. "Mr. Bascomb—" I began. I felt curiously like I was knee-deep in thyroid. We'd been in his office for about five minutes, and I realized I hadn't even introduced Colt.

"Sorry, baby." He leaned over toward me and smiled. It was the sweetest, most lovable smile I'd ever seen in my life.

"Mr. Bascomb," the speaker said, "I have the Coast on the wire."

"What do they want?" he said.

"You just asked me to get Mr. Karp, Mr. Bascomb. We had to reach him at home."

"Put him on," said Bascomb.

"Hello, baby," he said into the phone. "Sorry to get you up so early, baby, but we got a problem with the integrated commercial. The agency says the client says you can't say that about beer. It gives it a negative feeling. Yeah, it's all right for Bobbie to pretend to rub it on his hair; very funny, but he can't feed it to the dog... No, it's something about the SPCA. Well, read it to me. Uh-huh, I think they'll buy that." He flipped the speaker. "Gorgeous, will you get this on your phone? Take it down and send it to the agency."

"Yes, Mr. Bascomb," the speaker said. In a minute, he was off the phone. "Mr. Bascomb—" I began again.

"Gorgeous," he said to the speaker, "keep the calls off for a minute, will you?"

"Yes, Mr. Bascomb—but I've got a call from Dumont on that miniature setting you ordered."

"Give it to Johnson."

"I did, Mr. Bascomb. He says you ordered the set. He doesn't know anything about it."
I was beginning to feel that Bascomb was the kind of executive who never delegated anything to anybody.

"Make a note. I'll call Dumont back."

"Yes, Mr. Bascomb."

"And keep the calls off for five minutes."

"Yes, Mr. Bascomb."

"Well, baby," he said to me, giving me the smile again. "Mr. Bascomb," I said, "this is Mr. Fleming." They shook hands.

"I knew Temple would come around," Bascomb said.

"I tried to make that point clear, Mr. Bascomb. We haven't come here exactly from Standard-Idea. We're more or less on our own."

"You might say," Colt broke in, "we're sort of a subsidiary company. But your problem interests us a great deal."

"The problem interested Temple, too, baby. It was the time and the price he didn't like."

"We feel that we can take care of both those items," Colt said.

"That's good, that's good." He flipped a key on his speaker. "Baby," he said, "will you come in for a minute."

A rather heavy female voice answered, "Yes, Mr. Bascomb." He turned to us. "I think we ought to bring Miss Frye into this, baby. She's our research expert. Used to be with Gallup. I decided an outfit like this needed a research expert. It's the Hoopers and all that that make the wheels go around."
"Oh, oh." I said it under my breath. I didn't mean to. Colt looked at me. Bascomb looked at me. "What did you say, baby?" Bascomb said.

"Nothing. I mean, I said, 'good.' You certainly ought to have a person like that." Miss Frye came in. She was the coat and tie and low heels type, with freckles and a heavy jaw.

"Baby," he said to her, "this is Mr. Beecham, and Mr. uh–"

"Fleming," Colt said. He never did introduce Miss Frye. Generally, he seemed to call men "baby" and women "gorgeous." He just couldn't seem to "gorgeous" Miss Frye. She didn't seem to mind.

"Okay," Bascomb said, "make with the survey."

"Well," said Colt, launching into the sales talk he had practiced in our bathroom, "the first thing you have to do is to forget everything you ever knew before about surveys.''

Miss Frye was just looking at Colt, steadily and coldly. I saw a small slide rule sticking out of her pocket. Her breast pocket, if Miss Frye would pardon the expression. We might fhm-flam Bascomb with this kind of a razzle-dazzle, but I had my doubts about Frye.

"You're familiar, I'm sure," Colt went on, "with the radar survey system that CBS has pioneered. It utilizes, as you no doubt know, many small transmitter units attached to receiving sets owned by carefully selected radio listeners. A central unit picks up impulses from these little transmitters, and makes a record of the programs being heard by the sample audience. It gives an instantaneous rating."

"I don't like it," said Bascomb. "You oughta see the lousy rating we got from it on our giveaway show two weeks ago.''

"However," said Miss Frye, "the rating was later confirmed by Hooper, and the difference was discovered to be less than two per cent, a negligible error."

"Mmmmmm, okay, baby, go on."

"Well," said Colt, "you can see the obvious drawbacks in this system, just the same. The process is very expensive, it measures only programs tuned in, without any indication of like or dislike, it's controlled by the network anyway, and it can only be used for programs actually broadcast on the air." I had given Colt a thorough briefing.

"Yes," said Miss Frye, who understood all these things, and more.

"These drawbacks," said Colt, "are precisely the ones that have been eliminated by the-" he paused for a second, then said slowly, "the Psychoelectronic Correlator."

"The what, baby?"

"The Psychoelectronic Correlator. It stands in relation to the radar-survey principle as a television receiver is to a crystal set. This truly amazing scientific miracle was invented, almost stumbled upon, I might say, by Mr. Beecher here. (I nodded modestly.) It receives impulses directly from the human brain!"

"What do you think of that, baby?" Bascomb said to Frye. "Whose human brain?" said Frye.

"As far as we can determine," said Colt, "it receives a mass impression of aggregate public opinion within the continental limits of the United States."

"Everybody's?" said Bascomb.

"Everybody's," said Colt. "And instantaneously."

"Did you hear that, baby?" said Bascomb to Frye. "Yes."

"What do you think?"

"What is it," said Frye, "a ouija board?"

"It's electronic," said Colt. "It apparently receives the electrical impulses of the human brain."

"Say!" said Bascomb, plainly impressed. I could see already that I'dbeen right about the electronic angle.

"An electronic ouija board," said Frye, with a deadpan ex pression. "I'm sorry, Mr. Bascomb, but to me it just sounds like a lot of crap."

"I know," I put in, "I'd have said the same thing. You see, I'm a research man, too, Miss Frye. I've been supervising tabulations at Standard Idea for a long time."
"And," said Colt, "Mr. Beecher tested the Correlator against more than a dozen different national surveys. The results were almost identical."

"Honestly," I said, "I wouldn't have believed it myself."

"'What have we got to lose, baby?" said Bascomb to Frye.

"As I see it, twenty-five hundred bucks."

"Tell you what we'd like to do for you," said Colt. "Just give us a chance to make a test. Without any charge. Let us test anything that you can check later with any standard survey."

"No charge?" said Bascomb.

"No charge."

"Okay," he said. "Give 'em something, baby."

Miss Frye thought for a minute. Then she went, "Ah ha, ah ha, ah ha." It was almost a Lynn Fontanne laugh, but an octave lower, and nasty. "I think I've got just the thing," she said. "How about the big panel job?"

"Why not?" said Bascomb.

"Listen," said Frye. "The agency is doing a big research job on one of our recorded shows. It may cost more than ten thousand. They're going into twenty cities all over the country, and in each one they're setting up panels of two hundred cross section listeners. They play recordings of the show to these people. All of them have a little button they push which records whether they like or dislike parts of the show, and the totals are all registered on a curve."

"I know," I said. "Like the Schwerin system."

"Like that," she said. "It shows whether they like the show, and exactly what parts they like or dislike most, minute by minute. They'll correlate the twenty cities into a master curve to give a national picture. We're going to play three different shows to each audience, and get three different master curves. Got it?"

I nodded. It was a standard procedure, though on a larger scale than most.

"All right," said Frye. "If this gadget of yours will really do what you say it will, why couldn't you give us those curves? The agency has already been working a couple of weeks to set this up, and they should be playing the records in a few days. We should have the final results in a week." She paused for just a second, and looked from one to the other of us. "Could you give us your results, say, two days before that?"

"That isn't giving them much time, baby," said Bascomb.

I didn't know whether we could do it, but I swallowed fast and said, "If you can give us copies of the records today, we'll bring you our results first thing tomorrow morning."

"If you can do that, baby," said Bascomb, "you can have the other job, and the twenty-five hundred."

"If it checks," said Frye.

"If your results are accurate,"

"Ours will check."

"Ours will be accurate," said Frye. I knew they would be.

"Will you run out, baby, and see if you can find us some extra pressings of those three shows?"

"Yes, Mr. Bascomb." Miss Frye left, and I could tell by the glance she gave us on her way out that she felt sure she had put us, neatly and scientifically, behind the eight ball.

Bascomb was on his feet now, and pacing. In this office, I figured, there were about ten laps to the mile.

"You mean, baby," he shouted from the northeast corner, "that this gimmick will get everybody's reaction to anything?"

"Anything," Colt said. "As far as we can determine," I added.

"Without the people hearing it, or seeing it?" He was coming down the stretch now, head up and breathing easily.

"Absolutely," said Colt.

"Apparently," I put in, "it registers public opinion potential."

He reached us, and stopped dead still. "Then answer me this, baby. What are your gimmick's reactions to-sex?"

"It has no personal feelings one way or the other," I said. I thought of MacInnes, and hoped I was right.

"I mean," he said, almost quivering, "can it take a dame and tell me whether she's got it, or she hasn't got it, and how much, and for how many guys?"

I started to open my mouth, and closed it again. The enormity of the whole MacInnes idea was just beginning to hit me for the first time.

"I-I'm not sure."

"Why not?" said Colt.

"Yes," I said softly. "Why not?"

Frye came in the door with a flat corrugated paper box. "Here are the records," she said.

"Baby," Bascomb told us, ignoring Frye completely, "if you can find that out, come around."

"Maybe we'd better find out first, Mr. Bascomb, whether they can find anything out," said Frye. "Personally, I have my doubts."

I took the records. "We'll bring our results to you in the morning."

"Okay, baby," said Bascomb. "And make it good."

And as we walked out of Bascomb's electronic, neo-Colonial booby hatch, I thought I heard a very small voice down inside of me saying, "Beecher, Beecher, you're going to be sorry." And another one that seemed to add, "How pure, Beecher, how pure can democracy get?"

As far as I can remember, it was the first time in the MacInnes episode that

I'd heard them. And if they could have told me what was going to happen in the next few months, I think I'd have taken the Gimmick and blown it into bits. Colt and I went straight to a phone booth, down there in the Radio City Concourse, and called Macinnes. We were lucky. He hadn't gone fishing yet.

"Where you calling from, sonny?" he said. "Sounds like you're in a coat closet."

"I'm in a phone booth."

"Not workin' today, sonny?"

"I'm sick."

"Then get some place where you can stretch out. Phone booth's no place to be sick in."

'Tm not really sick. I'm playing hookey from the job. Look, Mac, I-"

"Didn't think you had it in you. How about goin fishin'? Off Bayside they're gettin' real nice flounder. We can go Dutch on the boat."

"Listen, Mac," I said, "this is important. I've got us a client. We make our first survey today. Can you corne up to our place this afternoon?"

"I just told you, sonny. I'm goin' fishin'."

"Tonight could be time enough, I guess."

"They got the boxing tonight," he said. "On the television. Besides, sonny, I thought this business all blew over."

"We were just trying to get a client. For weeks we've been trying to get one, and now we've got him."

"I don't know," he said. "I don't want to hurt you boys' feelings, but I've been thinkin' a lot the last couple of weeks. Guess nobody ever figures he's happy, till he gets past the time when he is-when he gets himself all snarled up, and looks back, and says, 'Those were the good old days, all right.' 'Well, sonny, I'm leadin' a mighty good life, and I guess you might say I'm pretty happy about it. Like my niece says, 'Uncle Mac, you're the happiest man in the whole United States.'"

"Did you talk to her about our plan?"

"My niece? That's right, she used to work for your outfit, didn't she, boy?"

"Yes." I'd been out with Peggy a couple of times since our theatre date, but I still hadn't talked about our scheme. I was pretty far gone about Peggy, and I just didn't want to spoil things.

"Well, you know," Mac said, "she may be right."

"But just think. On our first job we'll make twenty-five hundred. Your share for about two hours' work will be over seven hundred dollars."

"Mmmmmm." He was tempted. I could tell that. "Three hundred and fifty dollars an hour."

"No. She's right, sonny. I'm mighty sorry. Sure you wouldn't want to go fishin', though?"
Already I was getting an idea.

"Colt likes to go fishing," I said. "Maybe we could join you."

"Glad to have him, sonny."

"I'll put him on." I opened the phone-booth door. Colt was so close he was breathing fog on the glass.
"What's the matter?" he asked.

"He wants you to go fishing."

"Fishing! What the hell, Beech-"

"I just want you to keep your eye on him while I handle some important business."
So Colt went into the booth, and on this, our day of decision, he made a date to go catch flounder in the waters of Long Island Sound.

PULP CULTURE PRESS

CHAPTER SIX

Peggy didn't answer her phone. However, I knew she was out doing surveys and might be home any time, so I went to one of those little coffee-bearing movie houses. I absorbed two very small cups, black, a French picture that must have been made in 1934, and a surrealistic movie about a man who tore off the top of his wife's head. It was almost four when she finally answered and told me I could come over.

Peggy lived in a soot-colored building on Eleventh Street, three windows wide and five stories high. Once, no doubt, it was populated by bearded men in basque shirts and espadrilles, making free love, poetry, and bathtub gin. Now, like the rest of Greenwich Village, it wasn't populated by men at all between nine and five. They'd taken their business suits and well-shaved faces to midtown or downtown by subway, and in the hall, you fell over Taylor Tots, roller skates, and tricycles. Only the legend of the Village was left, resulting in occasional outcroppings of batiks, silk-screen prints, and peasant skirts in the A and P.

I walked up five flights. Peggy opened the door. "Pardon me, miss," I said, "I'm making a survey."

"I've already got a survey." Peggy looked as though she'd just stepped out of a shower. To me, there's something whole somely erotic about a woman who has just hopped out of a shower. Peggy smelled fresh and clean, and her skin was pink and glowing. What you could see of it, I mean. She was wearing a quilted housecoat wrapped snugly around her body. There were soft greens and browns in it, and I think I noticed for the first time that Peggy's eyes were the same color—a blend of soft green and light brown. All right, it doesn't sound pretty, but it was. I kissed her right there in the doorway.

"This," she said sweetly, "is developing into a nasty habit."

"Is it for you? I can take it or leave it." Smile when you say that, Beecher.

"I'd ask you in, but I'm not sure there's room for both of us. We can try it, anyway."

I'd never been inside her apartment before. The room was slightly larger than the studio couch inside it. There was a single armchair and a dresser. "Here," she said, "I'll close the kitchen, and you'll fit." She closed a door, and the kitchen, a sort of closet, disappeared. There was plenty of room. If you kept the dresser drawers closed, I'll bet another person could have got in there. We sat down together on the studio couch, and I had a terribly urgent feeling that if I didn't jump right into the business at hand, I might forget about MacInnes altogether.

SEX MACHINE

"Peggy, we need your help." When dealing with a strong-willed woman, the best thing is to give her the upper hand. You know, her strength and your weakness, like in the women's magazines. I confessed everything, the gimmick, the deal with Mac Innes---everything.

"You see," I summed up, "it isn't as though a big outfit like Standard-Idea were trying to take over your Uncle Mac. We're just a couple of young fellows with a big idea. In MacInnes we thought we saw a man with a real mission." I hoped I could arouse her mother-hen instinct. I was doing my best to be a baby chick. "And also," I went on, "we thought we saw a chance to bring true democracy to America."

"And to make a fast buck," she said, figuratively speaking, just as I was about to flutter in under her wing.

"Well, we may make some money, but the real issue is bigger than that. It's—it's bigger than all of us."

"Is it?" She did seem to be coming around a little.

"But right now, we're just scared. Tonight, we have our first chance to prove ourselves. And do you know, Mr. MacInnes doesn't want to do it for some reason."

"I know," she said.

"Maybe that's where you could help us. You must have a little influence with him."

"Uncle Mac does exactly what he wants." I think she believed that. Women, I've found, really think that when they push a man around, he's doing what he truly wants to do. Only without them he just didn't know what it was he wanted.

"Well, I was thinking," I said, "that you might be able to point out to him what real satisfaction he could get from this. Just think. By working only eight or ten hours a week, he could make as much as, say, a thousand dollars a week. A year of that, and he'd never have to work again."

"But would he stop? Honestly, Fred, do you think once you get into a thing like that, you'd ever be the same?"

"But he could stop. Any time. You could make him."

"Oh, no, I couldn't." She had that pure his-mind-is-his-own look.

"If you could get him to start, I'll bet you could get him to stop."

"Mmmmmm."

"And if you don't, Colt and I—I just don't know what we'll do."

"There's one other thing," she said. "Had you thought there might be a reason Uncle Mac can do what he does?"

"No."

"Could it be, maybe, that he's the only man who can feel what everybody would think about anything, because he's the only man in the country who doesn't really care what every body thinks?"

"He doesn't seem to care, does he?"

"He's the most independent man in the world."

"I suppose," I said.

"Well, then, did it ever occur to you that if he started to count on all that money, maybe he might begin to care what people thought?"

"No, I hadn't thought of that."

"Had you thought even further," she went on, "and wondered what might happen when he did begin to care? Maybe he wouldn't be able to do what he does!"

"That couldn't be," I said, but the thought was terrifying. For the first time, if it was just for a few seconds forgot that Peggy Maddox, fresh and pink and glowing, was sitting next to me on the studio couch, so close that our knees were touching.

"I think it could be," she said.

And then, while I was still shaking under the impact of the idea, the other one swept over me.

"Why-" I began slowly, "you've answered your own objections, haven't you?"

"How?"

"If what you said is right, Macinnes has his own built-in safety valve. If he ever begins to get worried or unhappy—if he ever gets really concerned about what people think, the whole thing might end, all by itself. He wouldn't be able to do it anymore!"

"I wonder," she said. It was a new thought to her, too.

77

"Give it a try, will you?" I asked. "Call him up this evening, and use your influence."

"Well—" she began. "Of course, it probably won't have any effect. Uncle Mac doesn't care what anybody thinks."

"Maybe," I said, "it's just that he doesn't care what every body thinks."

Peggy looked at me and smiled. It was a beautiful, fresh, friendly smile. Somehow, all thought of Macinnes vanished, and the only thing in the world was Peggy Maddox, whose knee was touching mine. I put my arm around her. Her lips (artificial coloring added) were full and ripe, and there was just a glint of red on top of her soft brown hair. I kissed her slowly and deliberately. It was as thorough as a sixty-seven-city survey.

"A nasty habit," she said very softly, and her body seemed relaxing.

In Topeka, and Spokane, and Springfield, Massachusetts, the returns were coming in. On the subject of toothpaste, vitamins, and magazine serials, the measured mind of America was making itself up. Take a room in Greenwich Village, five stories above Eleventh Street. Run a survey on it, and ninety-four percent of the population, rural and urban, would say that it was too small and crowded, and lacking in proper cross-ventilation. But they might not have noticed the rosy light of the afternoon sun, coming in through the skylight. And they wouldn't have seen, at all, an equally rosy glow in one Fred Beecher, whose heart was full, and whose mind was made up.

Colt and Macinnes arrived at our apartment at about ten in the evening. Colt was carrying a large black object that looked like a suitcase, and Mac had eleven flounder, wrapped in a damp issue of the Daily News.

"Nice and warm," said Mac. "That's what I like, a nice warm day." It was warm, nearly eighty, and old Mac was still wearing the tattered gray sweater underneath a suit coat that didn't match his pants.

"You got any place we can clean these fish?" asked Mac.

"Maybe you wouldn't mind running off this survey first," I said.

"Gotta clean the fish, sonny. You gotta clean fish and get 'em on the ice or they'll smell on you."

Colt looked at me helplessly and shrugged his shoulders. "I'll help," he said.

"Sonny," he said to Colt, "judgin' by the way you were baitin' hooks, I figure you'd be more harm than good." Mac looked at me. "Ha! This boy's a real fisherman, he is."

"I got four of the little buggers," said Colt.

Mac was rolling a cigarette with fishy fingers and unwrapping the flounder on what we laughingly called our kitchen sink.

"What's that?" I asked, looking at the black suitcase.

"A turntable," Colt said. "Do you think Mac is going to ab orb those records through his pores?"

I'd almost forgotten you couldn't play transcription records on a regular phonograph. They were big sixteen-inch disks, and they played at thirty-three revolutions a minute instead of seventy-eight.

"I phoned six guys this afternoon before I met Mac," Colt said. "We picked it up on our way back." Colt was opening and assembling it.

"You were lucky to catch us at Mac's apartment. We only stopped there for a minute."

"It wasn't luck," I said in a low voice. "We phoned every five minutes for an hour and a half."

"What in hell did you do, Beech?"

"We just had cocktails and dinner at some little joint in the Village."

"You feel all right?"

"Why?"

"I don't know. You look sort of unconscious. Listen, Beech, you're not going for this girl, are you?"

"Who, me? I'm the cold scientific type. It was just business, that's all." Colt may have noticed that my voice had a hollow ring to it. We had a wonderful, fabulous dinner, and I can't remember what we were eating to this day.

"Did you hear her talk to him on the phone?"

"Well, no."

"Weren't you taking a chance?"

"No," I said, "I'd trust Peggy Maddox anywhere." Colt snorted.

"She told me afterward what she said. She merely asked him to give it a try for a while. After all, she told him, he could stop any time."

"That I don't like."

"I don't either, but it's a start. And having Peggy on our side ought to help."

"If she's on our side as much as you seem to be on hers," said Colt, "we have nothing to worry about."

"How about the turntable?" I said. "Is it ready?"

"It's ready," he said, caressing the needle with one finger and making a crump-crump noise cover over the speaker.

The fish were all cleaned, and Mac joined us. All we needed was somebody to clean Mac. He smelled like a filet of flounder. "I explained everything to Mac," Colt said, sitting him down at the Gimmick.

Mac hunched over the control button like a skinny old buzzard settling down to something dead. Well, he was going to sit in judgment on radio, and maybe that was appropriate. Colt started the record. Fanfare.

"Wait a minute," said Mac, looking at his big pocket watch.

"What's the matter?" I asked.

"Two minutes and he'll be over."

"What'll be over?"

"Bob Hope. Don't know why, sonny, but I always get kind of a backlash while he's on. Mixes me up."

"There's always some program on," said Colt.

"You figger it out, sonny."

"Hope's rating is about twenty-five," I said. "That means around twenty million people are listening."

"What does it feel like?" said Colt.

"Ever feel somebody giggling behind your back? Like that, sonny." We waited a minute and started the record again. Mac pushed the button back and forth, and the stylus recorded it on our moving drum. Colt held a stopwatch in his hand and marked the minutes and half-minutes on the moving graph-paper, right alongside the curve. The lights on the Gimmick were off. We weren't trying to impress anybody. Fifteen minutes later, the record ended, halfway through the program, a variety show. We had a nice curve on our paper, up where people were having a good time, down where they weren't. Up, for instance, for a male singer who must have had the microphone attached directly to his tonsils and who probably seemed sexy to the ladies. Down for the commercial and for a soprano who sang the "Italian Street Song" in a worried voice. Up, unaccountably to me, for a comedian with a larynx like a sawmill and a perennial case of apoplexy.

"How'd I do, sonny?" asked Mac.

"We don't know," I told him. "And we won't know until the big survey comes in. We made a nice curve, though."

"How do you like the show?" Colt asked.

"Didn't mind the girl singer," Mac said. "Kind of fancy."

Colt was worried. "Look at the curve, Mac," he said. "You say you like the girl, and she's the lowest thing on the graph."

" *I* liked her, sonny. Looks like they didn't,"

"Why not?"

"Maybe she's too fancy. Might even be they didn't like the song. Maybe everybody's got a different reason, I don't know."

"You mean," said Colt, "what you like hasn't got anything to do with it?"

"Don't know, sonny. Guess my feelin's are counted, same as anybody else's."

So we started up the next record, and Mac leaned over the machine. As the minutes rolled around on Colt's stopwatch, a fifth of a second at a time, the United States of America (and no doubt an overflow from English-speaking Canada) voted silently and instantly on yaks and boffs and a barbershop quartet. At least, we hoped they were really voting. Whether they were or whether the whole thing was in the head of Victor Macinnes, we couldn't tell. And we didn't learn whether we were all wrong or all right not till Bascomb's survey came back eight days later.

We didn't realize it at the time, but we had already stepped off the cliff with Macinnes. From the moment Colt handed in our copies of the survey to Bascomb Productions, we were swept along by forces as inevitable as the laws of gravity. And there are many who might say that our direction was just as surely downward. Looking back on it all now, I'm inclined to believe they'd be right. After Mac left that night, we stayed up late to assemble a neat presentation of our graphs with lettering in India ink.

Colt brought the material to Bascomb Productions the following day and gave it, he told me, directly to Miss Frye. She must have told Bascomb about them very quickly because he tried to reach me at the office about ten-thirty in the morning. I know because Diana left the message on my desk. It was there when I came back from my ten-minute trip down to Lexington Avenue for coffee. What happened after that I can only guess. Knowing old thyroid-and-adrenalin Bascomb, he probably said to our operator, "All right, who else is there, gorgeous? Try Temple, will you?" He must have, because Temple called me in at about ten forty-five.

"Sit down, Beecher," he said. I sat. He looked rather sad. His hand was supporting his ponderous and now somewhat overcast brow. "Feel better?" he asked.

"Much better, thanks," I said, remembering that I had been officially sick the day before.

"I just had a call from Bascomb," he said.

"Uh-did you?" I could feel the blade of the axe on my neck. "He was very pleased with your work."

"W-was he?"

"Beecher," he said quietly, "I thought we agreed to drop this whole project."

"I tried to make it clear to Bascomb," I said. "I told him we were doing this on our own."

"You and Miss Maddox?"

"And a couple of others."

"He said something about electronics. What did you do—wire Miss Maddox for sound?"

"Something like that, yes."

"Who knows," he said, "maybe it's just screwy enough to work. Not to get accurate results, of course. You'll never do that. But the important thing in this business is to make some body think you're getting accurate results."

"They'll be accurate," I said, hoping now more than ever that they would be.

"You realize that I'll have to let you go, Beecher. I don't have any choice."

"Yes, I suppose." Well, there it was. I was fired. Off and on I'd thought of the things I'd say to Temple at just such a time. But he sat there, looking like a big, sad Saint Bernard dog, and I felt sorry for him.

"The company policy," he said, "is three weeks' severance pay. I'll try to get you more if I can." I knew he would, too. Temple was all right.

"Thanks," I said. "We'll need it. We may not be in the big money for weeks."

"In a way," he said, "I hope you make it."

"Why should you?" I asked. "If our system really works, it'll probably be the end of every other survey outfit in the business."

"I doubt it. But if you make a big enough splash, you might just happen to throw a curve to the whole system. Might be a good thing."

"I don't get it."

"I'm going to tell you something. I worked in a steel mill in Gary till I was twenty-six. I didn't graduate from college till I was thirty. I had a lot of time to think about what I wanted to do. 'What,' I asked myself, 'is going to be the most important thing in the next fifty years?' Some people thought our time would be known as the Electronic Era or the Atomic Age. But I didn't. I thought the key to any century or any time was the force that influenced people's minds. Like the early Christian Church, or the Renaissance, or the concept of evolution. And I finally came around to realizing what our time would be called five centuries from now. The Poll Era, or maybe something like the Pollar Age. It seemed to link up with the idea of the spread of democracy and the rise of the common man. On the surface, it looked like a good idea."

"On the surface?" I said.

"I was pretty thick in the head. It took me a long time in the business, maybe five years, to see what was really happening. And then it was too late. I had a family, and I had to stick with it."

"Are you sure," I asked, "that you're not just suffering from a case of last-- last-election-itis?"

"Just the reverse," said Temple. "I think last November helped."

"I don't see how."
"It showed there could be a mistake, and it threw people off guard. The real danger, of course, is not that we're inaccurate but that we're almost always accurate— and will inevitably become more and more accurate with the years. Being complacent because the polls missed once is like going to bed with a loaded gun because you know about one that didn't go off."

"What the hell," I said, "all we do is make sure people get what they want."

SEX MACHINE

"We make sure everybody gets tomorrow what the lowest common denominator wanted yesterday."

"How in the world can anybody find out what people want tomorrow?

"You can't," Temple said. At the time, I thought he was acting mighty foolish, doing a standard genius act. "You can't," he repeated after a long pause. Nobody asked for Shakespeare, Galileo, Goethe, the steam engine, or the radio. Before they happened, nobody on earth could even imagine any of them. And even if anybody could have imagined them, the surveys would have voted them down the first time around.

"You ought to take a rest," I said. "You look kind of beat up." And that's the way I felt as I walked out of Temple's office, leaving him in one of his trances. But that, of course, was before Macinnes, before the miracle of Victor V. Macinnes.

The next morning at seven, we were sitting in the control room of a radio studio in Hartford, Connecticut. I was bleary-eyed and sure that the whole thing was a dream.
But it wasn't. In fact, the wheels had been in motion even before Temple fired me.
When I reached home, about noon, Colt was lying on the floor, face up, with the telephone draped loosely across his mouth.

"Okay, Punchy," he said, 'I'll be up there tonight. Uh huh, meet you at the studio in the morning." Then he hung up, and I told him about Temple, and the job.

"Great," he said. We burned the ships. There's no turning back—into the wide blue yonder."

"Keep out of my wide blue yonder. All we burned was groceries. Where in hell are you going tonight?"

"Hartford. Corne along. You're a man of leisure now. You've heard of Punchy Slade?"

No I said.

"The announcer. You know, I was going to make a Lowell Thomas out of him. Sell him as a program package."

"The name's familiar," I said.

"He has a beautiful speaking voice. Sounds like a cello hitting a low note. The only trouble was, he didn't have any sense."

"Is that a disadvantage?"

"Yes. A commentator shouldn't be too smart. If he is, he'll just wind up on a Sunday afternoon spot with no sponsor. On the other hand, he has to have some intelligence. Not so he'll know what to say. That's usually dished out to him from some where. So that he'll know what not to say. Punchy doesn't know that. He doesn't even know enough to sneer in the right places."

"Then why do we go to Hartford?" I asked.

"I had an inspiration. This morning I got to thinking about MacInnes and that graph we made last night. Did it ever occur to you that if he can take a record that's already made and tell what's popular and what's not popular he could take a script before it's broadcast and tell you exactly what parts people will like or dislike? Sentence by sentence. Even word by word."

"Oh, no," I said, trying to fight myself away from the whole idea. And just the top layer hit me, too. That idea's like an ice berg. Most of it is underwater. Kick it around for a minute yourself. Close the book and look at the ceiling.

"Besides," I put in again, "we're not sure that Macinnes can really do it not till we hear from Bascomb."

"I'll take that chance. Now for this job, what we need is a guy with a beautiful, melodious, and authoritative voice-—but no sense. No brains at all. Like a blank, virgin sheet of the best bond paper. That's Punchy. Punchy, plus a good hack writer, plus Macinnes, and we'll out-Hooper Winchell in thirty-nine weeks. Know what Winchell makes? Ten thousand dollars a week."

"Stop it," I said. I'd heard Colt talk this way before. Funny thing, though. I'd never been scared like this before.

"All we do is make the biggest possible noise, find the rip roaringest gripes, prejudices, and cravings-and at the same time make the smallest possible number of people mad. Make everything seem like a whale of a controversy-but be sure everybody's on your side."

"I can name at least one instance in which that approach didn't work."

"Hell, we just want 'em to listen, not go out and vote for the guy!"

"Let's wait a while," I said.

"I've got to be in Hartford tonight."

"For one thing, all this will cost money. Train fares and—"

"Sure, and entertainment, and maybe a lawyer for contracts. Hell, Beech, we're standing on the front step of the U. S. Mint, and you don't want to put a nickel in the turnstile."

"We haven't got a nickel. I'm out of a job, remember? Call up Slade. Tell him we'll see him in ten days." So, as I said, we were in a radio studio in Hartford at seven o'clock in the morning. And at about fourteen minutes past seven, Punchy Slade (known to a few early risers in Hartford as Preston R. Slade) was just going off the air. He was sitting in a small studio at a table that held a microphone, his script, a glass of water, and a stopwatch. He looked rather Yale-y in a shapeless, Brooksy gabardine jacket, and his close-cropped hair, iron-gray at the temples, was not just trim and tidy but somehow invulnerable, as though it couldn't possibly be mussed. His features were regular and vaguely aristo cratic. People were to say later that he had an honest face, which usually means a blank one.

He finished his broadcast, a technical triumph of modulated phrases and pear-shaped tones. For the most part, he read stand ard press association tele-type material sandwiched between commercials for a department store. He did it all with the same air
of polite urgency. I followed Colt out into the studio.

"You did a graaaand job, Punchy," he said. His voice sounded flat and dead, the way voices always sound in a radio studio. They get lost in those little holes in the wall. Sometime, maybe on Judgment Day, all those words will crawl out of their holes, and the effect will be rich, mellow, and downright nauseating. "Glad you like it, Colt," said Slade, raising his chin and placing his hand tenderly over his vocal cords, the way you'd touch a Stradivarius. "Bit of a cold. The old tones weren't coming out quite the way they should."

"It came out fine," I said, knowing I was expected to.

"Thanks, Fred," he said warmly.

"That was an incredible story about the old professor and the girl stowaway," I said. "Really fantastic."

"Yes," he said gravely, "very tricky story. Most people would have said emer-eee-tus. E-mare-itus is correct you know. I looked it up."

"Pretty daring," said Colt, shooting me a heavily loaded glance.

"Worth it, though," I added.

"I'm something of a purist," he said. "Can't help it."

A cadaverous little man came in. He wore a rumpled suit, a black knitted tie, and a slightly soiled shirt. His face had a greenish tint.

"This is John Meacham," Slade said, introducing us. "He writes the script."

"Well, I string it together," said Meacham. "Most of it comes off the UP machine."

"How would you like to change all that?" asked Colt.

"Why?" said Meacham.

"To raise your rating, maybe get you a national sponsor and a lot of money."

"What agency you with?" asked Meacham.

"You aren't with any agency are you, Colt?" said Punchy, beautifully.

"I'll explain all that," Colt replied. "Where can we get a cup of coffee?"
We went down to a coffee shop in the hotel next door. We all ordered breakfast except Meacham, who had a whiskey sour. Colt explained the machine and told them how it could increase their audience. "The first thing you do," said Colt, "is cut down the straight news about fifty percent."

"What about Smith?" said Meacham.

"He's the station's program manager," said Slade. However, he never gets up early enough to hear us. And even if he did, I think we could fix it."

"How?" asked Colt.

"He also happens to be my brother-in-law." That explained to me how Punchy had the program in the first place.

"Then we're in," said Colt. "Save about five minutes a day for special material. A crusade, a controversy, anything that will make people talk."

"At seven in the morning?" asked Meacham.

"It won't always be seven in the morning," said Colt, "and it won't always be just Hartford." They liked that.

"At first," said Colt, "it'll be a hell of a lot of work. Mostly for Mr. Meacham here. Because we don't want just one controversy. We'll want, say, a half-dozen. We'll test 'em all, and just use the ones that rate the highest."

"You mean," Punchy said slowly, "you're going to make more people listen just by changing the words?"

Colt put his hand on Slade's shoulder and looked him in the eye very earnestly. "Punchy," he said, "we certainly wouldn't want to change you!"

"Thanks," Punchy said, a tender little throb in his voice. "The deal is this,"

Colt went on. "We don't want a penny of what you're making now. But we're going to have a contract drawn up giving our company twenty-five percent of any increases."

"Twenty-five percent!" said Meacham.

"Let me remind you," Colt added, "that Winchell makes ten thousand dollars a week."

"I do have a better voice than Winchell," said Punchy.

"More timbre," said Meacham, with a straight face and without telling how he spelled it.

"Of course," Colt said, "that applies only to money made in radio, television, or movies. If you should happen to get elected President of the United States, you could keep your whole paycheck."

"But you'd have to stop the program," I said, "and that would amount to a considerable cut."

"Money isn't everything," said Punchy.

"Bravo!" Colt shouted.

"Im not just saying that," Punchy added. "I really feel that way."

"Good boy," said Colt. "Now, the mechanics of this operation will be a bit complicated since you're in Hartford and our apparatus is in New York. Suppose we say that every evening you write up the test material and phone it into us. It won't be hot news—you'll still do that part in the morning. We'll tell you what material to use."

Meacham looked worried. "You said we might have to test a half-dozen different scripts, right?"

"Maybe," said Colt.

"I can't write a half-dozen scripts every night. Even if it'll make Punchy the President of the United States."

"Well," I said, "once we find out what clicks, you shouldn't have to. We might ride one controversy for weeks. Maybe just test a couple of alternate angles on it."

"And, of course," said Colt grandly, "you won't have to do the actual writing yourself very long. A staff of writers will do that. You and Slade will just decide on major policy."

Punchy beamed. "Major policy," he repeated. "Yes, I'd like to decide major policy."

"The way it looks to me," said Meacham, draining his second whiskey sour, "major policy will be untouched by human hands."

"Just the opposite," said Colt. "Touched by all hands, in the whole U. S. A."

"It's democracy," I said, still believing it.

"Is it really true," Punchy said, twirling his whole diaphragm, "that Winchell makes ten thousand dollars every week?"

"True, true," I heard Colt saying. It was 7:45 A.M., and outside the windows of the coffee shop, I could see the traffic beginning to flow in the streets of Hart ford, Connecticut.

Sleep, Hartford, sleep while you can, I wanted to say. MacInnes has murdered sleep, and therefore, Hartford shall sleep no more.

CHAPTER SEVEN

During the next week, we lived on a diet of chili con came, baked beans, Post Toasties, black coffee, and cigarettes. By the end of the week, I was looking around for cut-rate chili. "And we might," I suggested to Colt, "start rolling our cigarettes like Mac." It was morning, and we were sitting by our hearth, our fireside two electric hot plates in the kitchenette.

"Why?" he asked. "We're standing on the threshold of great wealth, Beech."

"I have nine dollars left, and your next allowance doesn't come for another week."

"I didn't know you had nine dollars."

"It may have to last us for weeks. If we can keep from paying any more rent."

"Forget it. Today, we're in the chips. I'm going in to see Bascomb."

"He'll let us know if any results come through."

"You don't understand salesmanship, Beech. I'm just cementing relations. And you'd better let me have the nine bucks. Just to jangle in my pocket. It'll give me a feeling of self-confidence."

So I gave him the nine dollars and presently bade him goodbye, clutching in my hands our last lonely little can of Gebhart's. When Colt came back early in the afternoon, he looked flushed and triumphant and smelled highly of dry martinis.

"We're in, Beech."

"Did the surveys come through?"

"Any day now. But I had a lot of luck. Got in to see Bascomb just before lunch. And what do you know? He had a lunch date blow up on him, so I got in there fast and before you know it I was going out to lunch with Bascomb himself."

"You lucky, lucky boy."

"We went to Louis and Armand's. Honest, Beech, right now, Bascomb and I are just like that."

"What did you talk about?"

"Well, people kept sitting down with us. All kinds of people—announcers, actresses, and script writers—up and down. Our table was something like the information booth at Grand Central. But Bascomb and I got on a very friendly basis." He reached into his pocket and pulled out a quarter and three dimes. And it certainly was lucky I had that nine dollars with me. Here, Beech."

"Thanks," I said.

"I went easy myself. Said I'd just had a heavy breakfast." So there we were, with our relations firmly cemented and our future secure, if we could live that long. That evening, Mac came out again. He'd been working with us almost every night for the past week, trying to give them a really hot issue in Hartford. Meacham had tried all kinds of things on Mac, from politics to baseball, and the best crusade we'd found so far was one about Giving Every Little Dog a Home. This seemed to go over nicely in Hartford for a couple of days until, presumably, every little dog in Hartford had a home.

Reactions generally had been encouraging. There were no ratings yet, of course, but they'd pulled some twenty-five letters. Of these, twenty-two were favorable (i.e., Mr. Slade was doing wonderful work, and did he know of any little dogs who wanted homes); one mentioned something about going out and throwing up; and another said the writer had given a little dog his radio; and another accused Mr. Slade of being a warmongering capitalist-imperialist.

Slade and Meacham were willing to do business with us since this was more letters than the program had received in six months. However, as Colt said, we had to find something we could Get Our Teeth Into. Meantime, we shuddered to think what the flood of telephone calls from Hartford, collect, were doing to our phone bill.

When MacInnes arrived, Peggy was with him after dinner time (not, accurately, after dinner). She had come several times before, and I hadn't objected at all.

"I just wanted to be sure," she said, "Uncle Mac could find your apartment."

"Damn sight harder, sonny," said Mac, "to find that joint of hers down in the Greenwich Village. Good thing I used to have me a girl down there. She was a real hot mama, too. Skin just like cream. Yessir, just like cream."

"You'd probably never find Peggy's place in the dark, would you, Mac?" I asked.

"Not in the dark, sonny," said Mac, looking out of the corners of his eyes. "You might have to take her home again." Peggy smiled at me. She had on one of those jersey dresses that cling pretty closely all around. I gave Mac a beer, our last can.

"Aren't you havin' one, sonny?" he asked.

"Not tonight, Mac. I'm watching the waistline."

"Me, too," said Colt. Peggy looked at us strangely, and just so she wouldn't think I was sick, I told her, "We're perfectly okay. We just ran out of money."

"Why didn't you tell me? I have plenty." She must have had a good four dollars.

"Thanks, but we'll make it. We're expecting a big check in the morning." Brave, smiling through tears, that was Beecher. We were out in the kitchenette, and she opened the icebox and the cupboard.

"Why, I'll bet you're hungry!" Just then, the phone rang. It was Hartford, right on schedule. "Hello, Punchy," said Colt. "Just a second till we hook up the machine."

The man at the radio shop had wired a pair of headphones to the telephone receiver so that Mac could listen. I sat him down at his little push button, gave him the earphones, and started the drum revolving.

"Okay, Punchy," said Colt, "you're on the air."

We were all quiet for a few minutes while Punchy read some script. Colt put his hand over the mouthpiece. "Anti-vivisection," he said. "How's it doing?" I looked at the line on the graph. "Mediocre," I said.

"It stinks, Punchy," said Colt. "The words, I mean. Not your delivery. That's sheer music. Do the next one." The line started snaking across the graph again, a little higher this time, but nothing sensational. Then suddenly, it went straight up. "Yipe!" I said.

"What happened?" Colt asked. "Look!" I said.

"Stop a second, Punchy!" Colt said. "Here, you take the phone a second." Colt came over to the graph. I went to the phone.

"Tell him to repeat that last paragraph," said Colt. "Punchy," I told him, "this is Beecher. Do that last paragraph over, please."

He started it with something about mothers. Punchy was in favor of them. Where would we be if we didn't have mothers? Preston R. Slade had a mother himself. "What the world needs is more mothers," he paused slightly—"in the United Nations!"

"There!" shouted Colt. "It went up again!"

"Hold it, Punchy," I said.

SEX MACHINE

"What'd he just say?" Colt asked.

"He said we needed more mothers in the United Nations."

"That's what he said before. Is that right, Mac, do you get a reaction out of that?"

"Does seem to tickle their fancy, sonny."

I heard another voice over the phone, talking a few feet from the mouth-piece. "Wait a minute, Punchy, what the hell are you reading there?" The voice came directly on the phone. "Hello, this is Meacham. I'm sorry. Punchy mixed up the pages. It should read, 'What the world needs is more mothers. The page ends with a certain sweet little lady I know— my own mom.' That United Nations line is from page two of the next story." I explained it to Colt.

"Give me that phone!" he shouted. "Look, Meacham, I know it was a mistake. It's the same kind of mistake that Greer Garson made before she discovered radium. We stumbled into something we can really get our teeth into."

I was glad I couldn't hear Meacham's reply.

"Where would Gabriel Heatter be if he was cynical like that? I think this has got something! Mothers- that's a great subject, but I'm a little tired. It's been overdone. But the switch is Mothers in the United Nations! Everybody likes the idea of the United Nations and peace. It's just that they get lost in the shuffle, and they don't understand all the ins and outs. No, you're right, I don't either. But tie it up with something basic like mothers, and it's natural. You should have seen it ring the bell with Macln... mean on our machine.   Hell, Meacham, I don't know what the story is. That's your job. All the delegates ought to be mothers, maybe. That might be it.

. . . Sure, especially the Russians. Everybody. And bring the kids. Kick it around a while.... Sure, call us again later if you get anything hot."

When Colt put down the phone, Mac said, "Sonny, that sounds to me like a lot of bellywash."

"Why?"

"You figure the people who listen to the radio in Connecticut pick out the United Nations delegates from Poland?"

"You don't understand the radio business, Mac," Colt said. "We don't care what anybody does. All we care is—do they listen to us, talk about us?"

Mac took off the earphones and shook his head slowly. "Sure is a funny business."

"You said it yourself," Colt added, "that the people in Hartford would like it."

"Who said Hartford, sonny?"

"I mean, you said people would go for it. Hartford people are no different. They'd better not be. I'm thinking about two hundred stations, coast to coast."

"Mighty funny business," Mac repeated. "Say," I said, "what happened to Peggy?"

"Thought I saw her sneakin' out a while back," Mac replied. "That girl's got an awful weak stomach when it comes to going's-on like this."

She was gone, all right, and it made me feel pretty bad. Here I was, falling in love with Peggy Maddox, and she just didn't seem to have the proper respect for my career.

However, in about ten minutes, the bell rang, and Peggy came in with a paper bag.

"Well," she said, "have you made Mr. Malik a mother?"

"You're as bad as Meacham," Colt said. "Hard, cynical. Just wait until you've done business for a while with the Great American Public."

"There's nothing. wrong with the G.A.P. that can't be fixed," she said. "You just take a kid and send him through the second grade all his life. You can't blame him for not knowing what they teach in the third grade."

"I don't know what that's got to do with it," said Colt.

"You will," she replied, taking the paper bag to the kitchenette.

"What's in there?" I asked.

"Something just like Mommy used to make. It would have been a lot more like it if there'd been something open besides the delicatessen."

She was taking a big stack of groceries out of the bag: green noodles, spaghetti sauce, mushrooms, Parmesan cheese, cans of beer, cheesecake, and lots of other things.

"Just stand there like that," I said. "I always want to remember you that way."

She held the green noodles, wrapped in cellophane, in front of her like a corsage. "I know," she said, "it brings out the green in my eyes."

"Lovely, lovely," I said. I'm sure Colt and Mac thought I was kidding, and I suppose I was, out loud, but somehow I was sure, for the first time, that Peggy Maddox, standing there in the middle of all that delicatessen, would make an ideal mother for my children.

"Mammy, mammy!" shouted Colt, breaking the spell. "How did you know we were hungry?"

"I have a gimmick," she said. "It's electronic, one hundred percent"

Two days later, after lunch, we were sitting in the frantic neo-Colonial office of Roger Bascomb. We were a bit lean, but not too hungry. The morning after our spaghetti dinner, we had discovered a ten-dollar bill, folded up and stuck in the machine, not far from Mac's control button. When we phoned him and tried to thank him, he just said, "Hell, sonny, don't know what you're talkin' about. Must have been left there by the U. S. Navy."

Bascomb's secretary called us the next morning and said to be there at two-thirty that afternoon. We were, and after a half-hour or so in the Colonial Kitchen waiting room, we went in.

"Hello, baby!" Bascomb said. "How you doin'?"

"Fine, thanks, Roger—" Colt began, evidently feeling that my nine dollars had won him certain privileges.

"I have the coast on the wire, Mr. Bascomb," the desk speaker said.

"Put 'em on, gorgeous," said Bascomb.

Five minutes later, after three telephone calls and four or five conversations on the interoffice system, he flipped a switch on the interoffice and said, "Come on in, baby, and bring those surveys."

Miss Frye came in with an armful of graph paper. I had been having nightmares in which Miss Frye had appeared in various forms, ranging from a freckled-faced English bulldog to an animated Mack truck. As she came in Bas comb's door, I thought that, on the whole, the real Miss Frye made them seem like a puppy dog and a scooter bike. Her underslung jaw was set at a fighting angle, and her haberdashery was as masculine as a coat of mail.

"Spread 'em out, baby," said Bascomb.

Miss Frye did, right on the floor. First, she put down our charts, which looked very neat in their black India ink. Then she spread out the agency's charts, which looked even neater, in India ink and three different sizes of varying type.

The curves looked quite different. Ours had high peaks and low valleys. Theirs were closer to straight lines.

"There must be some mistake-" Colt started.

"There's no mistake," said Frye, without emotion.

"You can see, baby," Bascomb began, "that they don't look much alike."

"However," Frye continued coldly, "if you'll notice the vertical scales, you'll see that each square on the agency scale equals five squares on the Beecher-Fleming scale."
"Cut the double talk, baby," said Bascomb. "I don't get it."

"It simply means," said Frye, "that if you translate these sets of charts back to figures and redraw them on the same scale, they will show a plus or minus variation of perhaps one to two percent."

"Is that good, baby?"

"Good?" said Frye. "I'm not talking about one chart; I'm talking about all six, for each fifteen-minute half of all three shows. It is not only incredible. It is absolutely impossible."

"Miss Frye means," said Colt, "that our results are so good she can't believe them."

"This," Frye continued, "is either the most fantastic coincidence in the history of public opinion research or it is the arrival of some kind of robot messiah." She sat down and lit a cigarette. "It's the god-damnedest thing I ever saw in my life."

"I can guarantee it's no coincidence," I said. "We've tested our system again and again."

"Geez, baby, if it's that good, I'll take a chance." Bascomb turned to Frye. "How's about those emcee records, kiddo?"

"I'll get them," she replied. "All I ask, Mr. Bascomb, is a chance to be there when they run the seance."

"We'll be glad to have you, Miss Frye," Colt said quickly. "Thanks." Frye went out.
"This is strictly routine," said Bascomb. "We gotta replace an emcee on 'Housewives Matinee.' You know, a women's audience show. We had these five different guys put in guest shots, maybe ten minutes apiece, and took off recordings. Who's the best guy, that's all I want to know, baby."

"We ought to be able to find that out for you tonight," I said.

SEX MACHINE

"Okay. It's worth two thousand bucks to me."

"You said twenty-five hundred," Colt said.

"We're ten days late. We gotta face it, baby, it's not worth so much now."

Colt stood up. There was a determined look on his fat, red face. "Once we set a price," Coit said, "we never change it." He actually started for the door. I got up, too. Colt had a lot of guts, I suppose, but I thought he was overdoing it.

"Okay, okay. Give me a break for trying, baby," Bascomb said. "Twenty-five hundred it is, and I'll give you a check for a thousand today."

I started to breathe again. "Frankly, kids," he went on, "this job isn't worth it now. The agency is chiseling down the price on the show already. I'm not saying radio is a dead pigeon. But let's face it, baby, television is the thing now. And what's gonna be the bread and butter of video?"

"Wrestling?" Colt answered.

"Sex!" said Bascomb. "Television will bring sex back into the home. And that's where you kids come in. I gotta master plan on sex, and I want to run a survey on it. The way I figure, baby, bazooms are on the way out."

"I don't know," I volunteered. "To me, they're basic."

"Legs were basic. In the twenties, legs were definitely basic, baby. Now, who looks at legs?"

"Me," said Colt. "I never look above the navel. Give me a babe with long, beautiful legs, preferably in sheer stockings and high heels, and I'm happy."

"' I'm talkin' about mass appeal, baby. I've got no interest in special perversions. Here's the theory. Why did legs become important? Answer, because nobody ever saw a leg before the twenties. A leg was dirty, baby. Then they got draped all over, and they got to be like elbows or the back of your neck."

"Not to me," said Colt, "but I follow the logic."

"Take it from Bascomb; the same thing is gonna happen to the bazoom. Sure, they'll hang on for a while. The only thing that would kill 'em dead would be a style to wear 'em out in the open. But remember, a lot of guys did some pretty shrewd buying while beautiful bazooms were a dime a dozen. How did they know what was coming? Luck, baby, sheer luck. But with you boys, I'm going to put this thing on a scientific basis. All I wanna find out is—what's next?"

"We can do it," said Colt.

"Wait a minute," I corrected. "If there's any opinion right now on anything, we can find it. But we can never tell what anybody will want, even ten seconds from now. And no other poll can, either."

"But we can spot a trend," said Colt.

"Spot me the right one, baby, and you'll be in the money." Frye came in with the records, but my mind was far, far away. I was trying to think how Victor Mac-innes, sitting in front of a pile of copper wire and old iron, was going to take the American Woman apart, like a frying chicken.

"Now, Fred," said Peggy, "I told you I didn't want another cocktail."

"They're only Manhattans," I said as two more settled in front of us.
We were in one of the grand old baroque hotels on Fifth Avenue, with its high columns, brocaded walls, dowagers with clipped poodles, and young ladies in mink jackets (even on this warm spring day). The men all looked as though they owned art galleries on Fifty-seventh Street.

"I am thirsty," she said, finishing a baby croquette of hot crab meat.

"Prettiest girl in the room," I said. And she was, even in the old plaid suit.
"You should have told me we were coming here; I'd have worn a dress."

"Poof. See that mink jacket. I will buy you a mink jacket like that, with a built-in poodle."
There I sat, with over two hundred dollars in the pocket of my three-year-old suit that cost thirty-two, including the extra pair of pants. Already the Manhattans were putting mink in my blood.

"Don't think you can buy me, Fred Beecher. Did you say mink?"

"Remember, you love me for my brain. You said."

"Fred—" She was suddenly trying to fight her way through the manhattans. "Where did you get all that money? From Uncle Mac?"

"For him," I said. "For him. He is now hanging in a hock shop. Tonight, we redeem him."

"I should choke on this." Peggy held up her drink. "Remember our deal. We were going to give it a try. This afternoon, we split a check for a thousand. To-night, for a few hours' work, we'll pick up another fifteen hundred. Come along. You can watch."

"Play it over again," said Miss Frye. "I wanna see the lights."

SEX MACHINE

"Let me freshen up your drink," said Colt, taking her glass. "Easy on the water," said Frye. We had a case of scotch, a case of bourbon, plenty of gin, and good French vermouth. We even had some new lemons. Mac had splurged, too. He had a brand-new Bull Durham package. He was sitting at the machine, with tobacco crumbs scattered happily around the floor and a half-glass of stale beer in front of him.

I started the last record again and tried not to listen. We had heard all five candidates for the job as master of ceremonies for this women's daytime quiz show. Number five was the jolly, fat, roly-poly type with a high-pitched giggle. Number one had been a fast-talking comedian, with a mental gag file and an automatic joke every time a woman opened her mouth; number two was an ex-announcer who sounded embarrassed; number three impersonated the clean young romantic lead with muscles in his voice; and number four, the winner, changed his pace rapidly from a tears-in-my-eyes golden wedding tribute to a you-devil-you attack, threatening to turn the "ladies" over his knee and spank them.

"Beautiful, beautiful," said Frye, letting a mixture of sixty percent scotch and forty percent water trickle easily into her underslung jaw. MacInnes was pushing his hand back and forth over the rheostat, and our Gimmick was a riot of flashing lights.

"Just wait," I said, hoisting a bourbon and soda. "When you get a rating of one hundred, it makes an American flag, nine feet wide, in red, white, and blue lights." I felt tremendous euphoria and power, as though we had, right in our hands, the key that would make us rule the world.

"Beautiful," Frye repeated, and then, after a long pause, she said, "but sad. So sad."

"What's so sad, girlie?" asked Mac, taking another swallow of warm beer.

"I like you," she said to Mac, irrelevantly. "Sad," she went on. "You remember about the cotton gin?"

"Sure," I said, "it took the seeds out of the cotton."

"Sad," she repeated. "Did the work of thousands, and thou sands, and thousands. What happened to 'em?"

"What did?" asked Colt.

"I don't know. Does anybody know?" Nobody knew. "Same thing's gonna happen to thousands and thousands. Know what? Taking polls is a major industry, yessir. Getting so that more people are asking questions than answering 'em. Panels, telephone, door-to-door, stop you on the street. The golden age of polls was coming." Frye drained her glass. "No more. Beautiful dream is ended. No more questions." She glared at the machine. "Everything's automatic."

"Give everything time," said Colt, "and it'll be automatic.'" The phone rang, and it was Hartford. Colt listened for a minute and then put his hand over the mouthpiece.

"For crying out loud!" he said. "They're having a parade. Two thousand mothers!"

"Where are they marching?" mumbled Frye.

"On the State Department in Washington, D.C.," I ad libbed.

"No," said Colt, his ear still in the receiver, "they're just milling around Hartford." He spoke on the phone.

"They did, Punchy? Seventy-thirty in the evening? How much? That's terrific!"

"How much?" I asked.

Colt ignored me. "Sure, we've got time, Punchy. I'll hook you up with the machine." Colt turned to Miss Frye. "Miss Frye," he said, "do you mind if we cut off this record for a minute?"

"Where's the parade?" said Frye. "All I want is to get in the parade."

I put the earphones on MacInnes, and for Frye's benefit,, I plugged a wire into the machine, too. I wasn't too careful. I knew that, at this point, as far as Frye was concerned, I could have plugged MacInnes into the machine.
"Okay, Punchy, shoot," said Colt.

Mac took another swallow of the stale beer, and bent over his push button. "How much money did he say, sonny?"

"A hundred a week more, Mac, and it's only a starter." Mac nodded, and the lights began to splutter and glow. I poured Frye another scotch, and went over to Colt. He spoke softly, one ear in the receiver. "Punchy's getting a new time. Seven-thirty in the evening!" he said. "It starts next week. And a new sponsor. Beer. Already there are rumblings in Bridgeport."

"I guess Punchy is very happy."

"He's a little worried. One of the women's dubs wants to make him a delegate to the United Nations."

"First," I said, "he'll have to become a mother." After that day, events moved along so quickly they frightened us. Well, they frightened me. Colt was in his glory. We gave Bascomb the results of our second survey, and he sent us a check for the other fifteen hundred dollars. We told him we were working on the sex angle.

"We're trying to determine an adequate test group for our preliminary survey," I said. That was research double talk, which meant you were temporarily behind the eight ball.

"Let me know, baby," said Bascomb, "and I'll send you dames by the dozen."

"Mmmmmm," sighed Colt. "We should specialize in this type of research." Macinnes, too, seemed enthusiastic about the project when we described it to him.

"You tell him, sonny, to send along a nice bevy of blondes. Kind of round, plumpish ones. With nice creamy skin."

"That's it!" said Colt. "I'll bet that's the trend, to more curves, to the ripe, full-bodied figure."

"Is that right, Mac?" I asked. "Would you say that the men of America are beginning to go for the heavier, more voluptuous type?"

"Hell, sonny, let the men of America do their own tomcattin'. I've been goin' for nice round gals since I can't remember when."

"Keep your glands out of this Mac," said Colt.

"I can tell 'em, sonny, but they've been talkin' back to me for fifty years."
I knew that we'd have to develop a more unbiased approach. But before we were able to neutralize Mac's glandular proc esses, we had a phone call from Cyril Manners, of Manners House.

"I say," he began, in a synthetic British accent, "I was up to Hartford last week visiting my sister. Met a fellow named Smith at a cocktail party. Stupid oaf. Owns a radio station up there. Let something slip about a fantastic automatic survey you fellows invented. Tell me he's lying, isn't he?"

"No," I said. Sometimes, I was to discover you could slip in a yes or no if you were quick about it.

"Is it true you can get instantaneous results?"

"Yes."

"Will you have lunch with me?"

A couple of hours later, Colt and I met him in the Cub Room of the Stork Club.

PULP CULTURE PRESS

The waiter brought us to his table, where he was sitting, read ing the Satur-day Review of Literature. He had no drink. Manners never drank. He stood up, and we could see he was rather short and thin. He wore glasses with huge shell rims. His features were finely chiseled, sharp, and cold, his hair thin and blond. He wore a shirt that must have been handmade, a Sulka tie, knotted precisely and exquisitely, and a quiet but obviously pedigreed glen plaid suit. We intro-duced ourselves and sat down.

"Really," Manners said, "how can you expect me to believe such a fantastic story?"

"We can prove it," said Colt, and gave names and dates.

"Please!" Manners stopped him. "Every good farce has a premise, and I'll accept it."

Colt was hurt. "This is no farce, Mr. Manners."

"Not yet, perhaps. Leave that to me. Tell me, first, have you any experience with the publishing business?"

"Not much," I said. "At Standard Idea, we ran a few surveys to pick titles for books."

"Ah, yes," he said. "The first step. The entering wedge. It might interest you to know that I've just had a survey made myself. Tested out one of our historical novels, in manuscript. Based on the results, we cut fifty-five pages down to two paragraphs, changed the ending, and sold it to the Literary Guild."

"Here, gentlemen, you have the first phase-the public with a blue pencil, the public as an editor, so to speak. I believe your device will lead us to the second phase-the public as a creative writer."

"But—" I started, "we can't do anything like that!"

"Nonsense. Hollywood is beginning to do it already. They've polled titles and endings for years. Now, they're sending their Gallups and Ropers to Peoria and Podunk for reactions to story ideas and situations. Would you like to see Gable and Turner on a raft? How about Bogart and Bacall as a psychiatrist and a lady acrobat?"

Colt had a faraway look in his eyes. It was roughly three thou sand miles away, in a westerly direction. "That's very interesting," he said.

"So," said Manners, "I'm going to let the public write a book for me. With your system, it should be quite easy."

"I don't get it," I said.

SEX MACHINE

"When I was fourteen, I sent away for a device that was guaranteed to supply story plots. It was simply a series of lists. Male characters, an Army captain, a beachcomber, a professor, and about thirty others. Female characters, an actress, a school teacher, an heiress, etc. Settings-say, a dock, a newspaper office, the Riviera, a college town. Complications, like 'because of mistaken identity a great injury is done,' and resolutions, such as a long-lost relative is found, and a misunderstanding is resolved. You shuffled these elements together, and presto, you had a plot."

"I never liked the plots. At fourteen, I was very sensitive. However, my plan is to use a very similar method." He handed us some typewritten sheets. "Had my girls go through a few dozen best sellers and take down types, settings, situations. Put my advertising agency to work, too. Had them list what they thought were sure-fire characters and situations. Brought in some freelance writers. Dipped into Polits Dramatic Situations. Made up a lot of it myself. I took a fast look at some of the lists. Characters: a passionate young Southern aristocrat; a beautiful innkeeper's daughter; the young wife of a newspaper magnate; a dashing Confederate cap tain; a matinee idol; a sensitive young sculptor. Dozens and dozens more. Settings: a plantation, a motion picture lot, the court of Louis XIV, an island in the Pacific. There were lists of situations and complications, too."

"Now my plan was," said Manners, "to get public reactions on each element, then put them together and get reactions to synopses. Step by step, on a national basis, it might cost millions."

"We could do it for you very reasonably," said Colt.

Manners had bought us two rounds of martinis. By this time, we were making good progress on the second pair. "Is it possible," I said, "to write a good book this way?" Colt kicked me under the table.

"Absolutely impossible," said Manners. "We will have a book that's a composite echo, signifying nothing and selling, I hope, five million copies."

"You certainly don't have much faith in the public," I said, raising my legs as high as I could: Colt kicked the leg of my chair so hard he nearly spilled his martini.

"Faith? I don't know," said Manners, smiling pleasantly. "I do know that I have boundless respect and boundless contempt for it. Professional respect and private contempt, I should say. And in that, I'm no different from the average inhabitant of what I call the Idea Belt."

"What's that?" asked Colt, playing straight man.

"It's an area about the size of a wheat farm, and in it are decided the bulk of the ideas that are distributed to the people of the United States. It's bounded roughly by Thirty-fourth and Fifty-seventh Streets, Lexington and Seventh Avenues. In it are most of the publishing houses of books and magazines, virtually all of the offices of the advertising agencies and radio networks, most of the theatrical producers, and even a considerable portion of the real controlling interests of the movies.

"This is the Idea Belt. Some ideas even start here. But most of them don't. They can start anywhere, but if they're going to reach the people, they must come here to be screened, measured, processed, often emasculated, and reissued in million lots. We add to them our little idea-selling ideas, the amusements and book sections advertisements, book jackets, fancy illustrated pages, and arrangements for seventy-five instruments. And we do it all with our ears to the ground and our fingers on our noses.

"The rent is very high in the Idea Belt, and whether we stay here depends only on sales figures, box office, best-seller lists, and circulation. So we vibrate like a fiddle string to every change in the opinion that, basically, we create. We give them what they want, and we go to every extreme to find out what they want, though we know all the time it will be only a varia tion of what we have already told them they want."

Manners was enjoying himself. He made his little speech without hesitation, as though he'd put on the same performance at many a cocktail party. "It is somewhat like," he said, "a man hitting a tennis ball against a barn. The way it comes back depends entirely on the way he hits it, and the way he hits it the second time depends pretty much on the way it comes back. But we don't see it that way, so instead of blaming ourselves, we blame the barn.

"So you see, gentlemen, I'm laboring under no delusions. Tell me now, can you take these lists and give me a true popular reaction on the different elements?"

"Yes," I said, "I think we can."

"How long will it take?"

"We could probably have them for you tomorrow."

"Good. Then, if I take these elements, give them to some writers, and have a series of sample synopses prepared, can you tell me which of them will be the most popular?"

"Absolutely," said Colt.

"And then, if I have sample chapters prepared, can you tell me which ones appeal most and which portions should be cut?"

SEX MACHINE

"Yes," said Colt.

"What will it cost?"

"Let's see," said Colt, as though he were thinking up the terms right then. He'd been talking them over with me since Manners' phone call. "I'd say about a thousand dollars for each different operation."
Thats a great deal of money.

"That would be just the advance. Since our organization would be, in effect, co-authors of the book, we would expect to share equally in the royalties."

"Not at all," said Manners. "The actual co-author, as I see it, is the American public. Your function is merely secretarial."

"Then," said Colt, "we're going to be the highest-paid secretaries in history. We want half of all the author's share, including, of course, the picture rights, radio rights, and all the rest."

"Utterly fantastic," said Manners.

"I don't know," Colt went on. "If the book's a flop, neither of us makes anything. If it sells five million and gets big movie money, we'll all make a fortune, including the people who do the actual typewriter work."

"Oh, yes," said Manners, raising his head dreamily and apparently forgetting all about the bargaining. "I almost forgot. I expect you to help me with the pictures on the front and the back of the jacket, too. The heroine will be on the front. I'll send you sketches. Want to see just how far you can go in the matter of breasts."

"A considerable distance," I said.

"And, of course, on the back of the jacket, we'll have a photo graph of the author. Want you to help me there, too. I'll give you twenty or thirty photographs. Powers and Thornton should have a number of excellent ones."

"Do they have pictures of authors, too?" I asked naively.

"Ah, youth," Manners said, looking at me kindly. "Beautiful girls have been in considerable demand lately, but I wonder. Who buys most of these books? Men? No, women, by two or three to one. Sometimes more. Perhaps a handsome, virile young man in an open-necked shirt. The Victor Mature type, possibly. Perhaps even the boyish, open-faced type, with a Van Johnson grin. It might bring out the mother in them. And I'll throw in a couple with bangs. Couldn't you test them all?"

"Just the pictures?" I asked.

"Well," said Manners, "I'll have to make sure they speak more or less grammatically. And of course, I'll have the model, whoever it is, read the book very carefully."

"We'll test them all," said Colt, giving me a pained look. "There'll be no charge. It'll be one of our services. We'll even survey your advertisements or publicity stories if you like."

"Yes," said Manners. "Yes. I believe you should. Well, in that case, gentlemen, I'd say your terms are still outrageous. But I think I'll accept them. I'll have a contract drawn up today."

"Good," said Colt, smiling sweetly.

"Yes," I said, but it sounded slightly strangled.

"You needn't worry, Mr. Beecher," said Manners. "The effect on American literature will be negligible. And the profits from our little confection will enable me to publish three or four small volumes of esoteric verse, which will sell three hundred copies to each of the people who can understand it. To say nothing of one or two very sincere and bitter novels by disillusioned Southerners."

That afternoon, Colt bought a car. We went up to one of the used car showrooms near Columbus Circle. It was last year's Chevy convertible, the speedometer read about 8,000 miles. The price was only two hundred dollars more than it cost when it was new. I had to admit it was quite a bargain. "But, remember," I said, "we don't have any real money yet." "Beech, you'll have to get overmthinking in small numbers. I'm being very conservative. There's a '47 Cadillac convertible up the street."

"What's stopping you?"

"They want too big a down payment." He made his payment in cash, but I noticed that most of it was in hundred-dollar bills. After he signed some papers, we drove the car right out, top down, with the radio playing.

"Look around," said Colt, pointing at the big office buildings hanging over us on both sides. "In all these buildings, people are cooped up, hot and miserable. You, too, Beech, would have been shut up in that cubicle on Lexington Avenue."

"My conscience would be a lot clearer."

"Why? You were doing the same thing. You just hadn't got to this stage yet."

"Ummmmm," I grunted.

"What's wrong with it anyway? Just giving people what they want, isn't it?"

SEX MACHINE

I grunted again.

"Forget it," he said. "I'll find a telephone. You can phone Peggy, and I'll try to find somebody, too. We'll go out to Jones Beach." We were lucky. We caught Peggy in between surveys.

"The beach?" she asked. "Oh, no, it's too hot for all that subway riding."

"Git next to yaself, babe," I said, in my own version of a New York accent. "Ya thinkin' of some other buoy friend. Weah gain' by cah!"

"By cah?" she said. "Geez, well aw roight!"

Colt made a few calls and finally located a girl who worked all weekend on a news magazine and was off in the middle of the week. We went to our place to get bathing suits, then down to the Village for Peggy. I went up to get her, and she was all ready, wearing slacks and a sort of T-shirt. She looked very fresh and pretty. I kissed her. In fact, I kissed Peggy quite a lot these days.

"You like?" she asked.

"Wonderful!"

"I mean me, in slacks."

"I like the shirt. It does something for you."

"Oh, stop."

"But the slacks—I don't know if Colt will allow a woman wearing pants in his car." We went down, and Peggy was very impressed with the Chevy. We drove on to the Murray Hill district to pick up Colt's friend Phoebe, who lived in a brownstone. When she and Colt came out the front door, Peggy nudged me and whispered, "Where does she think we're going?"

"Shhhhh! Colt likes her that way."

Phoebe was a slightly muddy blonde, eyes a bit too small and too close together, and a rather unpleasant giggle. However, she had the most beautiful legs in the world, long, straight, beautifully shaped, with slim ankles and small feet. Even for the beach, she was wearing 15-denier nylons and four-inch heels.

Phoebe looked at the car and said, "Oh, isn't that cute!"

We went down through the Queens tunnel, and after a few miles, we picked up Grand Central Parkway. Phoebe was in the front seat with Colt, legs crossed and skirts blowing. Peggy and I were in the back seat, very close together. "See?" said Peggy. "Everywhere you look, new houses are going up."

"Yep," I answered gloomily. They were nearly all alike, little square boxes with little square windows. "Here we are in the glorious postwar world, and they're building those dark, cramped little imitation Cape Cods. For the same money, you could build small modern solar houses, with plenty of glass, lots of light and air, and—"

"Why don't they do it?"

"Just damned stupid," I said.

"Don't make me laugh, Fred Beecher. When anybody builds five hundred houses like that, what does he do? He makes a survey. The survey says that's the kind of house that will sell."

"It's only because people have never been in the other kind. Let 'em live in a modern house for two days, and one of these dog houses will seem like a coat closet."

"Well," she said, "if nobody ever builds a modern house until the surveys prove people like them, how is anybody ever going to find out he likes 'em?"

Up in the front seat, Phoebe was squealing, "Oh, look at those little houses! Aren't they cute!"

"Regular little doll houses," said Peggy, very sweetly and loudly enough for Phoebe to hear her.

"You," I said to Peggy, "are trying to undermine my faith in democracy."

"And you," said Peggy, "are trying to undermine democracy's faith in democracy. I don't know why I ever let Uncle Mac help you." We moved apart slightly and began looking at the scenery. But as I sat there sulking, I couldn't help thinking that Peggy had brought up the matter of houses in the first place.

"Peggy," I said, inching over, "what kind of a house would you like?"

"Is this a survey? Are you after a mass reaction?" But she was smiling.

"I'm just taking a small sample. Urban females, aged twenty four, named Peggy Maddox."

"I doubt they'd have any opinion worth projecting on a national scale." But she started to tell me. She liked red brick and unpainted, waxed cypress and big glass surfaces and a wide, overhanging roof.

"Well, then," I said, "you'd probably build just about the same kind of house that I would." We were sitting close together, and her eyes looked very pretty, like early springtime in the woods, with little soft brown and green flecks.

"Peggy—" I started, trying to hold my voice steady, "had it ever occurred to you that it might be more practical to build just one house for both of us?"

"I sort of hoped," she said, "that it would occur to you."

Right beside me, a very womanly-shaped T-shirt was rising and falling, and somehow I had my arms around it and was squeezing it tightly. The car stopped.

"Beech," said Colt, "have you got fifty cents? I haven't got anything but a twenty."

The man at the toll gate was looking at us. "You're holding up the line," he said.

"The hell with the line," I answered, handing him two quarters. The car jumped forward, plastering us to the back of the seat.

PULP CULTURE PRESS

CHAPTER EIGHT

THE NEXT MORNING, I called Manners and told him we wouldn't be able to bring in the survey till the following day. "A little trouble with the machine," I said, not mentioning that we hadn't returned from the beach until after ten or that it had taken several hours more for me to see Peggy home and make sure she was all right.

"Tomorrow will be time enough," he said. "And by the way, do you mind if I drop around and watch?"

"Glad to have you," I lied. I called Mac. He couldn't come in the afternoon, fishing, or in the evening, when boxing was on television.

"Look, Mac, this may be the biggest thing yet. We're going to write a best-seller."

"Now we're gettin' too big for our britches. I'm a yes-and-no man, sonny."

"That's all we need."

"You figure on writin' a book with nothin' but yes and no?"

"That's right. If it works, we could make as much as, well, maybe half a million dollars."

"You feel all right, sonny?" But he finally agreed to come out in the afternoon. I phoned Manners' secretary and told her. An hour or so later, Bascomb called.

"Geez, baby," he said, "we gotta get moving. I'm castin' some dames for a television show. What am I lookin' for, tails, titties, or what?"

"We don't know yet."

"I'm gonna round up some samples. Couple of cab loads." I told Colt.

"Good," he said, "I've been thinking about the kind of gimmick we need for that job, and I believe I've got it."

"You mean a method for determining a trend in sex appeal?"

"Hell, no. That's your department. I'm thinking of the mechanics. What do you do when Bascomb brings over his girls? You can't just have Mac look at 'em. It's supposed to be electronic."

"I guess not."

"You wait right here. I'll be back in an hour." When he walked in, he had a big gadget with a bellows and a lens.

"What is it?"

"Part of an enlarger. You know, for photographs."

"I don't think Bascomb wants them enlarged. He wants them life-size."

"Nobody's enlarging anything. See, I got them to put a piece of ground glass on here. You focus it like this."

"The picture's upside down."

"I don't care if it's inside out. There's a thing here I can screw into the machine. Like this. How does it look?"

"Like a cover for Popular Mechanics."

"Then we're all set, huh?"

"All set. Except that I haven't the vaguest idea how we're going to do what Bascomb wants us to do."

"It'll come to you." It hadn't come to me when Madnnes arrived, about mid-afternoon. The temperature was climbing toward ninety, and, with the soggy New York humidity, Colt and I were nearly melted, even in short-sleeved shirts. Mac was wearing a heavy wool suit. Or, I should say, he was wearing pants from one suit and a coat from another.
"Take off your coat, Mac!" I said.

" 'Fraid to, sonny. Little bit drafty in here."

I had just had time to brief Macinnes on the best-seller prob lem when Manners arrived.

"Beastly weather," he said, throwing off his coat and standing in a beautiful white silk shirt before us. We introduced him to Mac. "How do," said Mac. "You the fellow who's gonna write the book?"

"Everyone," he said, "will write the book. My personal opinion, amounting to one part in a hundred and forty million, will no doubt be represented by one contemptuous comma."

We started right in. I read the items off the list, Mac slid the little button, and Colt read off the numbers on the scale. "A little girl from the slums." Lights up and down, red, blue, and yellow.

"Thirty-two."

"A beautiful and ruthless young noblewoman." More lights.

"Fifty-seven."

"I trust," said Manners, slipping on a pair of sunglasses, "that you are not indulging in any unnecessary pyrotechnics for my benefit."

"Look the other way a minute," I said. Then I read, "An ambitious and passionate little harlot." It was a regular aurora borealis. "Seventy-nine," said Colt.

"It might help if we reduce the ratio on the enumerator," I said.

"I don't see how you can," said Colt seriously, "unless you make a counter-balancing reduction in the distributor. They're on a parallel circuit, you know."

"It's a chance we'll have to take," I said, turning down a couple of lights. The phone rang. I picked it up.

"Hello, is Mr. Bascomb there yet? I have an important call for him-"

"No, he's not here."

"When he arrives, would you mind having him call his office?"

"I don't expect him here at all."

"Oh, dear. Didn't I call you an hour ago?"

"No."

'I'm so sorry. Mr. Bascomb told me to call and say he'd be there. With all the test material."

"You'll have to tell him he can't come now."

"I can't reach him. Please, Mr. Beecher, will you just have him call his office?" I'd just put down the phone when the doorbell rang. I pressed the button. I looked at Colt and Manners helplessly. "We're about to receive a shipment of the sexiest girls in the United States."

"Bascomb?" said Colt.

"Yes." I opened the door, and there was Bascomb, a shiny-headed little Bascomb in the sharp Broadway suit.

SEX MACHINE

"Hello, baby," he said, dancing like a soft-shoe routine. "I want you to meet the girls. Come in, Kids." They came in, all six of them. Blondes, brunettes, red-heads, in assorted sizes. Some of them had those black hat boxes, like photo-graphic models. One of these, a tall, slender, imperious brunette who probably appeared in Vogue, was dressed rather awkwardly in what I assumed was high fashion. One slightly plump blonde wore blue eye shadow and a dress that showed that her mammary glands were large, ripe, and unquestionably real. A tall redhead, who I later discovered was in the chorus at the Copacabana, was almost equally blessed and had, in addition, a pair of long and beautiful legs.

"Call off your names, kids," said Bascomb, and they did. We introduced Man-ners.

"Not the Manners House Manners?" asked Bascomb. Manners nodded. He looked a bit startled but happy. "I worked with some of your boys, baby. They sold me on
doin' one of your books on my 'Stump the Critics' show."

"Yes. Autumn Planting. One of my prestige books."

"Hmmmmm?"

"A good one, I mean. Lost money."

"I don't know how the guy could write, baby. I didn't read the book, but he loused up my show. Sort of a deadpan voice, with a squeal! And both the critics liked the book. No fight. Without a fight, you got a real turkey on your hands."

"Mr. Bascomb," I said, "your office wants you to call immediately."

Bascomb started phoning, and Colt fussed with the lens on his
optical gadget.

"Let's try,," I said to Mac, "to run off a few more of these book characters."

"Do my best, sonny," said Mac, keeping his eyes on the plump blonde, "but there may be some seepage." I read off a couple of character descriptions, trying to watch the percentages simultaneously. The lights started Bashing, the girls started giggling, and Bascomb talked louder.

"Kids," he shouted, one ear still to the receiver, "get your clothes off."

Squeals.

"You can go in the bedroom," said Colt.

"A beautiful young half-caste," I read. No lights.

"All their clothes?" asked Mac.

"Let's face that problem when we get to it," I said, and repeated, "A beautiful young half-caste." The rheostat went all the way up, the machine made a great flash like lightning, and all the lights in the apartment went out. Several girls in the bedroom screamed.

"What happened?" said Manners.

"You have to talk louder, baby," said Bascomb on the phone. I can't hear you."

"We blew a fuse," I said.

"It couldn't have been that good," said Manners. Colt ran to the fuse box on the wall of the kitchenette and bumped into three girls in lingerie fleeing from the darkened bedroom. More squeals.

"Mac," I whispered, "was that an honest reaction from the country as a whole?"

"Don't know, sonny. For a second, everything went sort of spangled." I looked at the scale, and it read one hundred percent. The lights came on.

"We'll try it again. A beautiful young half-caste."

"What's that, sonny?., asked Mac.
"A beautiful young half-caste!" I shouted.

"I don't know," said Bascomb, hanging up the phone, "if Powers has any young half-castes. How about giving one of these kids a pancake job?"

"We're talking about Mr. Manners' book," I said.

"And I think," added Manners, "we'd better put off our survey a while. Perhaps you'd like me to come back later."

"Stick around, baby," said Bascomb. "We got some stuff here that might go good in a book." The girls started coming out of the bedroom, wearing bathing suits. Mac looked disappointed.

"Where do you want 'em?" asked Bascomb.

"Line up over there by the couch," said Colt, focusing his gadget with the lens and the ground glass. "The actual procedure will be up to Beecher."

"Thanks," I said, wondering what would happen next. There was a moment of silence, during which everyone except Mac looked at me attentively and respectfully. After all, I was a man who knew how to separate the chaff from the wheat, the flabby from the voluptuous, the ugh from the oomph. Mac knew better. He just kept looking at the plump blonde with the well-filled mezzanine.

"First," I improvised, "let's try to get an overall picture. Step over here, girls, in front of the lens. One at a time." The girl from the Copacabana was first. She sort of flowed forward, in that oozing kind of walk that showgirls have. Colt swung the lens on her.
"Look!" he said to Bascomb.

Bascomb came around in back of the ground glass. "Even upside down she looks good," said Bascomb.

"Take a reading," I said. The lights flashed. I looked at the scale. "Eighty-two!" I said.

"What a Hooper!" said Bascomb. "It's better than a heavyweight fight!"

"It isn't a Hooper," I said. "It's all relative." The next girl stepped up, the high-fashion model. She wore one of those flouncy bathing suits that helped to hide her bone structure. She needed something to help.
The lights went up. "Eighty-two!" I read.

"They're both eighty-two?" asked Bascomb.

"I can't understand it," I said, throwing a cue to the next girl. She was a redhead, very red, wearing one of those French bathing suits that look like a bra and a G-string. As she undulated toward the test position, her tail assembly wagged back and forth like a pendulum with the hiccups. Colt, Bascomb, and Manners looked at her fondly, with a definite drool in their eyes. But just then, I noticed Macinnes. He still had a finger on his little button, sitting in an elliptical slouch like a carrion crow. But he wasn't looking at the redhead. He was staring right at the blonde with the cantilevered front porch, and I had a feeling he'd been doing it right along.

"Take a reading," I said. Once more, the lights glowed, and again I read, "Eighty two." During the whole reading, Mac's eyes never left the blonde.

"They can't all be the same!" shouted Bascomb.

"They could be," I said.

"Maybe for different reasons," Colt added.

"However," I continued, "I think we have a statistical error. We're getting a group impression with all the girls in front of the machine. I want all you girls to go back in the bedroom and come out one at a time." There was more squealing and talking as they went back, and under cover of the noise I said to Mac, "I saw you, you old lecher. You were watching the blonde the whole time."

"Real nice, sonny," he said. "Got skin just like cream, yessir."

"Tell me this—what did the eighty-two stand for? Does that mean eighty-two percent of adult males, rural and urban, go for her?"

"Don't know, sonny. When you take a good long look at that blonde, do you think of adult males, rural and urban?"

"Listen, Mac, this is important! Keep yourself out of it! This calls for selfless service!"

"Dammit, sonny," he said, getting up, "I told you I shoulda gone fishin' today."

"Let's go, baby," said Bascomb. The girls came out individually, and the blonde was eighty two percent. The others varied, ranging from thirty-seven for the girl in the fluffy ruffies to eighty-six for the one from the Copacabana, the one with the obvious advantages.

"So what?" said Bascomb. "I'd pick 'em in that order myself, baby."

"So would I," added Manners.

"I wouldn't," growled Colt, staring moodily at girl number five, score forty-eight. She was no better than average above the neck or even above the waist, but she had perfect legs and wore sheer black tights and very high heels.

"Ummmrnm," I grunted, my attention having been dragged in several directions at once. What you really want is a trend, yes?"

"Right!" said Bascomb. "What'll they go for next? A gorgeous belly button? A beautiful little tail?"

"There might even be a complete revolution," said Manners. "They might start looking at faces again." We had one big window in the front of our living room, which was hung with a Venetian blind more than six feet high. I'd been thinking about it for some time. "Give me a hand with this, Colt," I said, jumping up on the window sill. We had it down in a minute, and hung it over the doorway leading to the bedroom.

"Here's the idea," I said, standing back from it. Suppose we're testing shoulders." I turned the slats so that only my shoulders could be seen.

"Let's give it a try," said Colt. "Come on, girls, we'll test out legs first."

"Why legs first?" asked Bascomb.

SEX MACHINE

"I'm just starting at the bottom," said Colt. "We'll work our way up!" First we tried the blonde with the chest. She giggled, "Why, nobody ever looks at my legs!" She was right. With her equipment, she could have been cut off at the hips, and sixty percent of the population wouldn't have noticed.

"Twenty-two!" I read. The girl from the Copacabana rang up forty-one, and the one with the tights, forty-three.

"So what?" said Bascomb. "You're te!lin' me one of these kids has got better legs—right' Geez, baby, I can tell you that myself."

I grunted again.

"How's about givin' me a montage?"

"A montage?"

"Run 'em through fast, one, two, three, four, five, six. Gimmie a fast impression of legs."

"I don't know if the machine can handle them that fast," I said.

"The Hell? This things automatic ain't it?"

"We'll try" said Colt. "Come on, girls, we want you to run around this way..."

The doorbell rang. When I opened the door, it was Peggy. I remembered then that she was supposed to come up for cocktails. We thought we'd be all through with Manners by this time.

"Freddie!" she began, "what's happening?"

"It's just business," I said and tried to introduce her to everybody.

"Okay, baby, let's make with the montage," said Bascomb.

"The what?" Peggy asked me.

"Just sit there and watch," I said.

"Okay, girls," said Colt, "start running around in a circle from here to here. Stop in front of the blind, here, just long enough to do a little business with your legs."

"Whatta you want," said the girl from the Copa, "sort of a bump?" She did one very expertly.

"Ah, research," said Peggy.

"Lower than a bump," said Colt. "A bump won't show."

"It isn't meant for show," said Manners.

"More like t is,'' said Bascomb, doing a buck and wing.

"Don't stop", said Colt.

"Geez, baby," said Bascomb, giving us the most lovable smile in the world, "I can't do any more of that routine with out a straw hat."

"Let's go, girls," shouted Colt.

They started running around, and Colt pretended to keep the lens on them.

"Forty-three! Forty-one! Thirty-eight!" I called out.

Mac stood up. "Dammit, sonny," he said to me, "you figure this is a lightning calculator?"

"I—fold it!" I said. The girls stopped. And just then the phone rang.

"I'll get it," said Peggy. "Electronic Surveys, good after noon!" She turned to us. "It's Mr. Slade, in Hartford."

"Tell him to call back," said Colt.

"He says it's very important; They're going to do a broadcast over the whole Yankee network."

"Give me that!" snapped Colt. "Hello, Punchy! ... Tonight? For crying out loud, why didn't you tell us before?... Yeah, I know we were out yesterday. We were making a survey out on Long Island. Look,'' he said, turning to Bascomb, "how about letting the girls rest for twenty minutes or so. We've got to check a script. It's going on the whole Yankee network."

"Geez, baby," said Bascomb, "what's a little New England hook-up? I got two shows on CBS tonight and one on NBC, not counting a Boston to Baltimore TV hook-up. I gotta get back to the office."

"Well-" Colt started.

Manners stood up. "Since this is my time, gentlemen, perhaps I should have some say in disposing of it."

"Hold on a second, Punchy," said Colt to the phone.

SEX MACHINE

"Just finish the first montage, baby," said Bascomb, "and gimme a quick test run on the bazooms. Ten minutes is all. Come on, girls, run through it once more." The girls began to dance around.

"Hold it!" shouted Colt. "Look, Punchy, we can't give you enough time right now for the whole script. Maybe we can call you later…. Okay, we'll try." Colt turned to me. "He just wants to get a reaction on the basic idea."

"What is it?" I asked.

"He says," Colt began, "that Mothers in the United Nations is getting to be a tired issue in Hartford. He wants to test whether they should go on to grand-mothers or get a new gimmick."

I told Colt, "Let's try hooking them up for a second."

"Hello, Punchy. Stand by for a minute, we're going to connect you."

Colt connected the telephone to the earphones and plugged a dummy line into the machine.

"Geez, baby," said Bascomb, "you got separate connections? How about run-ning both of them. Together?"

"And perhaps," said Manners, "I could just sit here and read my material aloud."

"Im serious," said Bascomb.

"Put the cans on, Mac," said Colt, handing the earphones to MacInnes.

"Ready, girls?" shouted Bascomb.

Peggy grabbed my arm, "Fred, if you don't stop them, I will."

"Action!" shouted Bascomb. The girls began to mill around. Manners held his lists at arm's length and sang out, "A beautiful young half-caste! Repeating, a beautiful young half caste. Over."

"Punchy!" Colt screamed into the phone, "louder, Punchy, louder!"

"Stop it," I bellowed, "stop everything!" Nobody heard. "More action, girls," yelled Bascomb. "Make with the legs, kick!" The girls kicked, and they squealed.

"A stark-naked young Hottentot," Manners ad-libbed, throwing aside his list, "with a sixteen-cylinder Cadillac. What am I offered? Sold, American!"

"Louder, Punchy, I can't hear a word you say!"

Mac put down his earphones and turned toward the door. Colt dropped the telephone. "Mac!" he called.

But Mac was already moving toward the door in his usual slouching shuffle. He half turned to take a last look at the blonde with the well-defined contour lines, but he didn't stop. By the time he reached the door, everybody was quiet.

"Now wait a second, Mac—" I began.

"Sonny." he said, "the way you're goin', you'll burn out a tube on that machine, and then where'd you be?"

"Try it once more, Mac," Colt begged. "We'll take things one at a time."

"Told you boys I was goin' fishin'. Should have stuck to it." He opened the door.

"Just stay for half an hour," I said.

"No hard feelin's," Mac said. "Be seein' you." He stepped out and closed the door.

"Good for him!" said Peggy.

"Go after him, Peggy," Colt wailed. "See if you can bring him back."

"I'm going after him," she said, looking straight at me, "but I'm not going to bring him back. Goodbye." She walked right out.

Know how you feel in a nightmare when you can't move your feet? That's how I was for about twenty seconds. Then I ran to the door and down the stairs. I reached the street in time to see Mac's car pull away. Both of them were in the front seat.

CHAPTER NINE

AFTER THE second martini, I said, "Maybe she's home by now." Colt looked at me wearily. "You just called ten minutes ago." So I called again and rang ten times. One would have been plenty. In Peggy's apartment, you couldn't get more than arm's length away from the phone if you tried. There wasn't any answer at Mac's place, either.

"You know," I said, "she does have a point. I don't mean just the confusion and getting Mac upset. There's a moral issue".

"Nuts."

"No, I mean it. It's a matter of integrity."

"Nuts. Every time anybody starts to get in the chips, integrity raises its ugly head. It's getting to be part of our folklore. If we were grubbing along in an attic, you'd call this a noble experiment in the interest of pure democracy."

"It's a great power we have," I said, pouring another mar tini, "and it seems we should use it to do some good."

"You mean we should juggle the answers and give people what they don't want?"

"I don't know, I still think Jefferson was right about the people, yet—" I trailed off. It was very confusing, and the martinis weren't making it any clearer. So we finally went out and had dinner at a little air-conditioned place in the neighborhood. Then I called Peggy and Mac again. No answers. I remembered that Mac had said something about watching boxing on television, so he was probably at some bar in Jackson Heights. "Let me borrow the car," I said.

"Take my advice. Stay away from her tonight."

"I am. At least until I see Mac."

"Okay, but be careful. We've got a lot at stake." So, at about eleven o'clock, I walked into Mac's apartment. "Come on in, sonny," he said. His coat was off, but he wore his ratty old s\veater, the sleeves pushed up above his elbows, like a college girl. "You sit right down. I'm just washin' out some things." He went back to the kitchen, which was right off the living room, and filled the sink with soap suds. "Just clear off that chair and sit down, sonny," he said.

It was an old Morris chair, and in it were copies of the Wall Street Journal, the Daily News, a tin can apparently full of bait, an empty beer bottle, and, over everything, a generous layer of Bull Durham. I cleared and sat. There was another old leather chair, also full of debris, a couple of straight chairs, and a studio couch with a tangle of unmade bedclothes on it.

"Where's Peggy?" I asked. "You take her home?"

He wrung out a shirt. "Yep. I took her down to her place. I don't think she stayed there, though. I figure she wound up in one of those French-speaking movies they have."

"She thinks all this business of ours is upsetting you, Mac."

"Me?"

"She thinks it's making you unhappy. Honestly, Mac, I'm sorry about this afternoon."

"Why? Wasn't mad at you, sonny. Wasn't really mad at anybody. Just got to feelin' like a scrambled egg."

"We'll never let them gang up on you that way again."

"First time since the old days," he said, "that I got that kinda tight feelin' in my stomach. Did I ever tell you about the old days, sonny?"

"Peggy said you used to work in a bank."

"I did. Now you'd figure to look at me that I was happy in those days. Wasn't. Well, with my wife I was, but except for that, no. Guess I was no different from everybody all over. Livin' a life of what Mr. Thoreau called 'quiet desperation.' All day, every day. And then when she left, well, I started to see me the way she must have. Peggy tell you about that, too?"

"She said your wife left you a volume of Thoreau and a timetable."

"Never did figure the timetable, whether she meant I was livin' like one or whether it was just a hint to move along. Maybe both. Anyway, I took the hint on both counts. Left town, and threw away my watch.

"Even tried livin' in a shack like Mr. Thoreau, but it didn't work out for me. The main idea, sure, but not the shack. Bein' simple like that's too complicated. You take a cup of coffee. Whole day's work, haulin' water, choppin' wood, buildin' fires. And lonesome, too. No sir, for a few hours' work a day, I can't get my simplicity piped into the kitchen and the bathroom. And I got people all around. I figure old Henry'd double-check that."

"I thought you didn't care about people, Mac."

"Sonny, I like people one at a time, two-legged humans you on say hello to, not 'people' the way you mean, in thousand lots. Big difference."

"Why don't we drop the whole thing for a while, Mac. You go fishing tomorrow."

"Supposin' I decide to get in my jalopy and go off for a couple of weeks."

I had a sudden empty feeling. "Well, Mac," I said, "we couldn't do a thing about it. You can stop any time you want. But if you stopped for, say, two weeks, we'd have to start from scratch. And that might mean a loss for the three of us, maybe a quarter of a tnillion in the first year. You can buy an awful lot of simplicity for that."

"Mmmmmm," said Mac, corning into the living room. He brought a couple of cans of beer, just the cans, with those triangular holes in the tops. "Have a beer, sonny."

"Thanks. I'm not fooling, Mac. We could build Slade up to a national spot in maybe six months and net for ourselves as much as a thousand a week. We could make almost anything off that book for Manners. Up to a million, with movie sales."mMac eased himself into the old leather chair.

"And that's not all," I went on. "Think how much there can be in this Bascomb deal."

"Sure was nice, sonny, lookin' at that blonde. Filled out her skirt so nice and full. But you keep that Bascomb fellow away. Don't know what it is, but he gives me the stomach flutters."

"He gave us our start, Mac. I know he's a screwball, but he's after something big. He wants a key to sex. I've been thinking a lot about it. What he wants is a trend, and I think the only way we can get it is by making a series of tests on the same group of women over a period of, say six months."

"Tell you what, sonny. I'll play around with your other stuff, but you get ahold of that Bascomb and tell him we can't help him." He wasn't mad, but he was mighty definite.

"You happen to see the boxing tonight on the television?"

"No."

"Well, sonny, it was the doggonedest thing. This little black kid, he got knocked down in the first round. But he got right up and—" Mac started in and told me about every fight. Took him two cans of beer to do it. That is, two for me, and one for him. And when I left, I was sure of two things: Mac hadn't changed his mind, and I had to see Peggy Maddox, or bust.

SEX MACHINE

Later I was knocking on Peggy's door.

"Who's that?" I knew I should have called.

"Fred."

"I don't want to talk to you."

"All right, then I'll talk through the door." I felt very humble then. I wanted to grovel, to crawl on the floor. I'm just putting that down so you'll know that what I did, that savage, un-Beecher-like action, wasn't premeditated. The motive for that deed must have lain dormant in my genes for centuries. The door opened.

"I warn you," Peggy said, "you're going to have to go right home." Peggy looked just the way she had that first afternoon—pink and clean and fresh. She must have taken a lot of showers.

"Peggy," I began, "you don't need to feel that way. I talked to Mac, and he said—"

"I don't care what he said." Suddenly, it started to sweep over me.

"Neither do I!" I said, whipping off my glasses with a single swift stroke of my hand, like a knight raising his visor.

"Fred!"

"I don't care what Mac said," I snarled. You know they say Helen Hayes can make herself look seven feet tall on the stage. Well, at that moment, Beecher was seven feet tall. Maybe taller. "I don't want to apologize. I don't want to discuss it."

"Fred!" she repeated, stepping back. I advanced one pace and slammed the door. "You can't do this, Fred, you can't—" I grabbed her around the waist and pulled her in. The house coat opened a bit, and I could see that she didn't have anything under it. I kissed her on the lips hard.

"Scream if you want to," I said. "No one will come."

"How do you know they won't come?"

"Go ahead." I don't know what I would have done if she had. I stuck my hand right in her hair and grabbed a handful. I pulled her head back and kissed her again. She tried feebly once or twice to close the housecoat. Somehow, I got the impression her heart wasn't in it. In closing the housecoat, I mean.

"Once in every man's life," I hissed (I think I hissed), "comes the time when he has to break the news to his wife."

"His wife?"

"Yes, you're going to be my wife, and you may as well face it."

"Yes, dear," said Peggy.

At this point I'll draw the curtain. There's a real Message in this story, and I want to be sure they hear it everywhere. Even in Boston. When I got home, Colt was still up. I told him what happened. The Macinnes part.

"Great," he said. "We're still in business."

"What about Bascomb?"

"Listen, Beech, I've been thinking. Since you left, I've been thinking about Mac and the ratings on those girls. Why in hell are we wasting our time figuring out a trend for Bascomb? Do you happen to know what's the biggest money-making operation in Hollywood? Not acting, not directing, not producing. It's the talent agents, the flesh peddlers. Some of those boys have fifty to a hundred names in their stables, and on each one, they're getting ten percent of a thousand to five thousand a week. You figure it out."

I did a quick calculation without slide rule, and it came to as high as fifty thousand dollars a week. "The hell with trends," he went on, "and the hell with pushing around a half-dozen babes. Why not take Mac out in the open, and let him give us a quick reaction to a thousand dames? Take a swing around the nightclubs, the musicals, the casting agencies, maybe even the cat houses."

"How about the Gimmick?"

"We can say we've got portable equipment. We can even make a gadget if we have to. For preliminary studies, we say. We just bring 'em here for the final check-up."

"You think Bascomb will like it?"

"Beech, I don't give a damn whether he likes it or not. Our other stuff will bring us enough capital to run this ourselves. His organization and contacts will help us a lot, though, and if he wants to split commissions with us—"

"He'd never do it!"

"That's a matter of selling. I'll see him tomorrow, I can convince him that we can double his income in a year." So we went to bed. Colt was humming happily to himself, and in his head, no doubt, were visions of sugarplums. Sugarplums with long and beautiful legs, walking over acres and acres of crisp green paper bearing high numbers and the pictures of presidents.

SEX MACHINE

As for me, I kept seeing the look on Peggy Maddox as she watched an untamed savage advance toward her. A savage named Beecher, that is, who was seven feet tall.

☆   ☆   ☆   ☆

From our seats at the bar, we could look up and see the girls. They danced in on a chromium-plated runway over the heads of the bartenders. "Just take your time, Mac," said Colt. "Look 'em over."

"Mighty pretty," said Mac, "mighty pretty." In fact, Mac himself was mighty pretty. We'd persuaded him to put on matching coat and pants, and we'd had them pressed.

We'd bought him a new shirt with a fresh, crisp collar, but we'd made sure it was size 16, for his skinny size 14½ neck, so that it hung on his shoulders like a shawl or a yoke for oxen. He said he didn't mind wearing a collar if he couldn't feel it. "Look at that blonde, sonny, the one with the nice creamy skin." You could see plenty of it, too.

"What's the reading on her?" asked Colt.

I took out my notebook. "Number 11," I put down. "Golden Garter." We'd been to ten other nightclubs, starting on the East Side and working our way toward Broadway.
"Is she the one?" I repeated.

"She's the one for me, sonny." He lit a match, and his Bull Durham flared up like a roman candle. The girls kicked their legs and did modified bumps and grinds. One girl had tassels on her bra, which she spun, first clockwise and then counter-clockwise, by an ingenious and appealing movement of her anatomy.

"Concentrate, Mac," said Colt.

"I am, sonny," said Mac, following the blonde with his eyes and no doubt sending powerful neurological impulses to what ever was left of his glands.

"Look at all of them, Mac," I said. "Where's the girl Bascomb is after?" The day before, Bascomb had made a compromise. He had agreed, with his characteristic serenity, to drop his original project and split his commission with us. Colt said the session was like a combination Kansas tornado and atomic explosion. But he'd succeeded in getting Bascomb to compromise. Bascomb Productions would stay out of our way if we'd produce one sample girl with Absolute Sex, one real powerhouse capable of unhinging libidos, rural and urban, coast to coast.

Mac tore his eyes from the blonde with the skin, and let them drift slowly

130

over the eight or ten girls on the runway. After a minute or two, he said, "The redhead." "Is she the one?" I asked.

"Best one here. sonnv."

"What would she rate, roughly?" asked Colt.

"Mmmmmm. Eighty's too high. Seventy's too low. Middle seventies, somewhere."

I wrote down, "Redhead. About 75." A scrubby little fellow on the other side of me said, "What do you like in the fifth?"

"Hmmmmmr The fifth," he said, his Racing Form folded to the past performances. "I got 'em all doped out but the fifth."

"Oh," I said, but he was already looking over my shoulder. "Redhead? You mean Redtop, buddy, in the fourth, and personally I think he's a dog. Strictly a dog and you won't get any seventy-five to one neither."

"It isn't a horse."

"A dame?" he asked, looking up from his dope sheet to the runway. "Geez, buddy, she ain't a day over thirty-five."

"What was the blonde at the Fifty-two Club?" Colt asked. I turned a page. "Eighty-six," I said.

"Let's go then," said Colt. "I'd like to turn up something that's ninety before the evening's over."

"I'm goin' too, buddy," said the horse player. "With you guys around. I'm gonna get my grandmother off the streets." We went to four more places, but we didn't find anyone over ninety, so I felt pretty discouraged. Mac was undaunted. "We'll turn up somethin', sonny."

"Are you sure you'll know her when you see her?"

"Can't tell till we see her." As for Colt, he found the girl with the tights, singing "Falling in Love Again" at a joint near Eighth Avenue. She was swinging her legs around, a la Dietrich, and it was more than Colt could stand.

"You go on," he said. "I'm going to try to get a date."

The next day Variety came out with the first story about us. SLADE SOCKOED BY SUPER HOOPER HARTFORD BREAKFAST GABBER PREEMS OVER YANKEE NET

SEX MACHINE

It told how Slade, until recently a small-time early morning news commentator, had been given an evening spot with a new sponsor and had finally earned a premier over the New England network. Much credit was due, Variety said, to a new system of electronic rating pre-testing originated by Electronic Surveys. The Gimmick was invented by two fellows named, they misspelled, Flemming and Beacham.

That afternoon we had a call from the New Yorker, the result of which, a few weeks later, was a stinging little paragraph in The Talk of the Town from the Eastern story editor of M-G-M, who just wanted to confirm the story, and said he'd get in touch with us later, after he checked the coast; from the research department of an advertising agency, which wanted to know how much it cost to subscribe to our service (we said we had no subscription list-we just did special jobs); and from the president of another agency, who wanted to see us immediately. Colt answered that last call and said we'd be down right after lunch.

"We can't," I said. "Manners is coming down after lunch for a final session." We'd had one other session with Manners, after our first rather hectic one, and we had just one more to go before his writers could take over the pre-tested outlines for the opening chapters.

''I'll call him," Colt said, "and put off the book session till later this afternoon."

"Remember, at four, we're due at the Broadhurst Theater." A producer was holding tryouts for a Broadway musical, and Bascomb had fixed it for us to look over the applicants. "Dammit," Colt said, "we'll have to do it this evening."

"Manners won't like it. And neither will Mac."

"You take care of Mac," he said, dialing Manners' number. When he reached Manners himself, he said without preface. "Look, Cy, we know how important this session is to you. We'd like to set the machine up ahead of time for it. Well, say eight o'clock.... Sure, you can make the show, you'll be out of here in twenty minutes."

So, at two-fifteen in the afternoon, we walked into the chromium and old pewter reception room of Meander and Swarm, an advertising agency that occupied six floors of a block-wide" building on Madison Avenue. At the reception desk was a lovely little old lady with a halo of snow-white hair and a slightly nervous expression. When we told her we wanted to see the president, Mr. O'Flaherty (and when she spoke to his secretary and learned he, would see us soon, she gave us a look of loving-kindness such as only a mother gives her son.

We sat on a beautiful Colonial settee, I whispered to Colt, "If O'Flaherty is president, what happened to Meander and Swarm?"

"They retired, with millions. You've heard of Wilson Mcandeder.

"Is that the same Meander?"

"The same." He took these cigarettes and tapped the package. He'd never smoked them before, but I noticed they were the same as the brand in the Lucite case.

"He took these cigarettes from nothing and made them one of the Big Three. When he retired, they made him ambassador to Bolivia."

A heavy, red-faced man with glazed eyes got off the elevator, nodded to the receptionist, and walked a bit loosely back to the offices. "An account man," Colt whispered.

"How do you know?"

"The slightly formal get-up, the heavy jowls, and the confused look from having had lunch, including about four old fashioned, with the client." A moment later, a potbellied, harassed young man in shirt sleeves trotted across the reception room, a pipe in his mouth, a pencil, and a sheaf of paper in his hands.

"A copywriter," said Colt, "I'd lay ten dollars on it. And in those two characters, you have the opposing poles of the advertising agency business, the 'contact' man and the so called 'creative' man." A thin brunette, who seemed to have a perpetually frightened expression, said Mr. O'Flaherty would see us now. We followed her back to a corner office. It was as big as a gymnasium and looked something like one. There were no paintings, only a few photographs, including several of the Cornell crew of 1925. O'Flaherty was in the back of a table. As we entered, he stood up and roared in a voice that sounded like a public-address system at a football game, "Hello, boys, come right on in!"

He was over six feet tall and must have weighed two hundred and fifty pounds without looking fat. His hair was close cropped and bright red, and he had baby blue eyes set in a very Irish face. There were two other people in the office. One was the copywriter we'd seen before. The other was a thin, tight-lipped fellow whose face was so pale it was almost blue.

"And this," roared O'Flaherty, making the introductions, "is Joshua Portal— Josh."

I shook hands with the pale gentleman, a firm hand, but ice cold.

"Josh is the one who told me about you."

"I saw it in Variety," said Portal quietly, underplaying O'Flaherty. "I double-checked Hartford. It seems to be true."

"It is," Colt said.

"Josh is going to hate me for this," O'Flaherty roared, "but the first thing I'm going to do is use you against him. Well, kinda." He beamed at Portal. "Gimme those commercials!"

The writer, who wasn't saying much, handed around copies of commercials. His hands were shaking. The scripts were ap parently typed up in quadruplicate, and he made sure that the original went to O'Flaherty.

"If you want speed, oh yes indeed—" O'Flaherty began. "Where did this come from?"

"It-it's a jingle—" the writer began. "We have some music for it. It's a sort of rhumba rhythm that—"

O'Flaherty swept it aside. "What's the next one?"

The writer handed around copies of another commercial. "Listen to that motor. Sound effect of motor. There, you'll see what a really fine gasolin—-" He broke off. "Look," he bellowed, "I don't get any excitement out of that. This is a new product. I want something like-'Man, you just never in your whole life ever saw; myt hing like this gasoline.' This isn't a copy, you understand, but I want that feeling. I want to get right in side 'em and make 'cm feel something."

"Well, Mr. O'Flaherty," the writer began hesitatingly, "after our last meeting, I roughed up something along those lines."

"Lemme see." He grabbed the commercial and began reading. "Man! You never saw anything like it! There's no other gasoline in the world like the new inmproved Air Line Gasoline—" He beamed, and went on reading the whole commercial, with emphasis. "Try this truly amazing sensational new gasoline —today!" he ended. He looked around from one to the other of us, his blue eyes dancing.

"Uh-beautiful," I said when he stared at me.

"What I want you to tell me," he said, looking at both Colt and me, "is this. Will that commercial sell?''

"We should be able to give you a clear idea," said Colt. "How about a rough idea now?" O'Flaherty asked.

"Now wait," I began, unable to hold off any longer. "We can take this copy back with us, if you want, and compare it with any other pieces of copy you have. I think we can give
you an analysis of which one the public will like the best, but I'm not sure we can tell you which one will sell the most gasoline."

"Well," said O'Flaherty to the writer, "get all these mimeoed up, and we'll run a test on 'em." The writer went out, clutching the papers. O'Flaherty narrowed his little blue eyes and looked shrewdly at us. "What does it cost you to do a survey like this?"

Colt looked back at him coldly. "About three cents' worth of electricity," he said. "We don't charge you for that. We're selling a service, and we will sell it exclusively to one agency. To you, if you want it, because you came to us first."

"How much?"

"It's a percentage," Colt went on. "One percent of total billing of whatever you use our service on."

"You mean," roared O'Flaherty, "if we use your gadget across the board on, say, twenty-five million dollars' worth of billing, you get two hundred and fifty thousand dollars?"

"Yes," said Colt.

O'Flaherty stood up. "That's the damnedest thing I ever heard of! An agency doesn't make much more than one percent clear profit on billing these days!"

"With our system, you would," said Colt. "You could eliminate almost your whole research department. And we believe you could almost eliminate a new business department, because, very soon, new accounts would come in faster than you could handle them."

"Completely out of the question," stormed O'Flaherty. "I'll give you a fee of five hundred a week for the first two months, on a test basis. Then we'll see what we can work out."

Colt stood up. "That's our proposition."

"Well," shouted O'Flaherty, "you know where to reach me if you change your minds."
"
Yes," said Colt sweetly, "and thanks very much for seeing us." He shook hands with O'Flaherty and Portal, and I did the same.

"I'll see you gentlemen to the reception room," said Portal. Somehow, that sounded a little unusual to me, and I won dered about it, till we were halfway down the corridor.

"Will you step in here a moment, gentlemen?" asked Portal, showing us his office. We walked in. It was much smaller than O'Flaherty's but quite large as offices went, with two big windows. The Venetian blinds on them were drawn, and the room was dimly lit.

SEX MACHINE

A secretary came in with a milk container, which she poured into a glass.

"Pardon me, gentlemen," Portal said, taking the glass. He opened the drawer in his desk. In it I could see a number of bottles and pill boxes. He put a couple of pills in his mouth and washed them down with the milk. "Just an occupational disease," he said. I remembered what Colt had told me. The quiet ones got the ulcers.

"Do be seated, gentlemen. Now, as you may have gathered, I am the account executive in charge of the National Oil Refining business. Also, if you have kept your ears close to the ground, you may have discovered that a number of other agencies have begun to solicit this account. Some have suggested that this has been encouraged by the National Oil people. And I've even heard—from the rumor mill, that if I were to form my own agency, I could take the account with me."

We hadn't heard any of this, but it was the sort of upheaval that was routine in the advertising business.

"Be that as it may," he continued, "I felt that unprecedented measures were called for, and that is why I suggested your names to O'Flaherty. However, after our meeting, I question whether your services will be utilized to such an extent that the situation will be remedied before it's too late. Suppose that a new agency were to be set up. What could you offer?"

"Everything," said Colt. "Within five years, it would be the largest agency in the country. We can do what any survey can do, at a fraction of the time and cost, on things like package and product design. We can do what no one else can do in creative research.

"Creative research?"

"We can go through your advertisements not only in the rough layout stage but, if you like, line by line. We can do the same with radio-not just commercials, but shows, ideas for shows, and parts of shows, from individual musical numbers to separate events."

"How do you know," Portal asked, draining the last of his milk, "that the Slade case wasn't a coincidence?"

"We're sure about that," I said. I briefly told him the whole case history, right from Standard-Idea through Manners, editing the Standard-Idea part to make it all seem electronic.

"I know Bascomb, of course. Do you mind if I call him?"

"We wish you would," said Colt. "Call Manners, too, at Manner's House. And we'd like very much to show you our machine. A small white bulb glowed dimly from time to time, in place of a phone bell. Never more than three times. After that time, we supposed his secretary took over.

"One thing," said Portal. "I don't think your one percent charges are excessive, if you can do what you say you can do. Not for an established agency. However, they might break the back of a new one."

Colt had been doodling on a piece of paper. "I was just thinking about that," he said. "Say we'd be willing to take a chance on a new agency. Not charge any fee at all till it made a profit."

"Yes?" It was very soft, almost a hiss.

"Like any gamblers, we'd expect more if we won. A percent age of the profits."

"How much?"

"One-third." He looked at me, and I nodded. If it really clicked, such an agency could make a million a year.
"That's too much."

"Normally, sure, but this agency's profits should be twice as high as the average."

"Well," Portal conceded, "it's true you wouldn't have to spend much money for creative people. As a matter of fact, nobody worth his salt would work in such a setup."

"You wouldn't need 'em."

"The farther you go with polls," I said cheerfully, "the less anybody needs to be creative."

"I'll have to admit," said Portal, "that the idea of an agency with a minimum of creative people appeals to me. Let me think over your proposition and, of course, investigate you thoroughly." He smiled a very thin smile.

CHAPTER TEN

Going out of New York is like going upstream on a river. You start on the mainstream, the parkway, six lanes wide and no stops. You branch off to a double-lane concrete strip, and off that to macadam or crushed rock. When the pebbles were rattling against our fenders, and the low branches were whipping the aerial, Peggy leaned back and said, "My, this is pretty."

I won't say that Peggy had been eating out of my hand. She was too much of a strong-willed girl for that. But I will say that our relations were much more serene. Two days after our talk with Portal, I borrowed Colt's car, and we were rolling north through Westchester. Peggy looked particularly fresh and full and ripe in one of those peasant outfits. You know, a bright-colored skirt and a little white blouse with drawstrings.

"This is what you need, Fred. Peace and rest. All of you have been going too hard."

"Maybe you're right."

The narrow gravel road was winding around one side of the Kensico reservoir. Now and then we could see water, with trees coming down to its edge, like a mountain lake. "Look in there," Peggy said, "it's almost dark!" On the reservoir side was a pine forest, so thickly grown that it looked black. I parked the car and we walked in, bringing the old beach blanket from the turtle-back, a shoebox full of lunch that Peggy had fixed, and some cans of beer, still cool. We spread the blanket on a thick matting of brown pine needles. It was soft, springy, and fragrant.

Peggy sat down, and before I knew it my head was in her lap and she was stroking what she probably thought was my fevered brow. "Just relax, darling," she said softly. Looking up, I could see her face, just beyond the beautifully rounded hills in the foreground. Under my head I could feel a gentle pulsing in her firm, round thighs. It was a most pleasant setting. "You're not relaxing. Stop thinking about the old business."

"What business?" Just then I couldn't think of anything but Peggy, and she was all mixed up with the scent of the pine needles. Then we were lying side by side, and I felt we'd been there for ages, and the trees had grown up around us. And for just a little while, the man from HQ kept ringing and ringing. All over the world, there was nobody home. "Let's just stay here," I said, "and never go back."

"Maybe they won't let us. I saw a sign. New York City Watershed."

"We'll shed water. You wait and see. It'll roll off us like a duck. You know,"

I went on, "I'll bet you could buy a lot around here. Be a nice setting for that house."

"Yes."

"And the way things are going now, we could build it any time. We finished the first part of the Manners job yesterday, and he's sending us a check—and from now on, Slade will come through with a couple of hundred a week for us, and Portal is figuring on an advance against profits, and—"

"Fred! You promised not to talk business!"

"Maybe that's the whole trouble with our age. You start to talk about love, and that leads you to talking about a place to have it in, and that leads you right to money."

"I don't know. It just seems like an awful thing to build a house on, this whole business with Uncle Mac."

"We may not have to, for very long. The way Colt figures it now, we could retire for life in a couple of years."

"A couple of years?"

"That's another thing the lawyer's trying to work out."

"No, I mean, what will two or three years do to you, and Mac, and-and-"

"And who else?"

"Maybe everybody else," she said, "in the whole United States. Did you ever think about that?"

"Yes," I said. I was thinking more about it all the time. But just then, with Peggy beside me in the pine woods, I was willing to let the United States take care of itself.

Within the next forty-eight hours, we conducted six preliminary surveys for Portal, on package designs, layouts, radio commercials, and the recording of a half-hour variety show. For Slade, we went over a whole series of scripts, and considered the proposition of making him into a "participating" program nationally. This would mean selling him locally or regionally to advertisers nationwide, who would cut in for their commercials in their own areas. Slade fan clubs were already beginning to blossom around New England; there was talk of nominating him for (a) Mayor of Hartford (b) Governor of Connecticut (c) United States Senator, and even a little loose chatter about "Slade for Fifty two," on a non-partisan (or one-party) ticket.

For Manners, we had made a detailed blueprint of a best seller. We selected the period, the Civil War, and the locale, a border state. We had lined up a complete cast of characters, including a heroine who was beautiful, sensitive, understanding, and over-sexed and a hero who was handsome, virile, domineering, and a bit sadistic.

We had even selected, from many samples, a style of writing that was most popular. Apparently rich, flowery, colorful, and "literary," it was as easy to understand as True Story or the Daily News. It adhered to most of the principles set forth by Mr. Rudolph Flesch and contained short sentences, short words (with a minimum of suffixes and prefixes), and plenty of personal references. It appealed entirely to the emotions and rarely to the brain, going like a sandwich to the midsection.

Having determined a style, we culled Manners' flock of writers to find the ones who could imitate it. For Bascomb, our task was more difficult. By this time, we had looked in on most of the Broadway musicals, had attended two tryouts, looked over the field at Equity, a half-dozen casting offices, and a few dozen more nightclubs. We even called a few numbers that Bascomb gave us and spoke to some personable young ladies who were apparently loitering, as the papers say, for the purpose of prostitution. They, of all the girls we approached, seemed the most outraged by our quest. For a price, they would be willing to sleep with us or provide us with a number of ingenious ways to pass the time, but our proposition seemed somehow unsavory.

"I don't know," said one blonde, who claimed to have a degree from Duke University, "it sounds immoral to me." In fact, we had quite a list, but Mac wasn't satisfied. "Will you ever be?" Colt asked him.

"Don't know, sonny."

"I mean, if you saw her, would you know it just like that and say "she's it!'"

"Could be if there is such a girl. How do I know? Maybe she's driving a tractor in the middle of Iowa." So it was lucky for us that things worked out the way they did because a complete survey of tractor drivers, car hops, B-girls, and high-school seniors, from coast to coast, would have been difficult without fitting Mac up with radar.

As it was, we were all dog-tired, so we decided to take a whole week off. Mac called up somebody on City Island and chartered a small motor cruiser. The man said there'd be room in one cabin for the three of us, plus another cabin for guests. I called Peggy, and Colt called the girl with the tights. She and Colt had become close friends—bosom friends you might say, if you don't know Colt.

So it happened that on a warm, beautiful Friday afternoon, all five of us were rolling over the Whitestone Bridge to City Island. Five of us, including Miss Lollipop Smith (so christened by a model agency; her real name was Emma). Peggy and I were nestled snugly in the back seat. We watched old Mac turn his gaze momentarily from Miss Smith's partially exposed underpinnings to the equally well-proportioned towers of the bridge.

"Mighty pretty," Mac said. "Got a nice clean reach to it."

"Of course," said Miss Smith, recrossing her legs. I realize it has won architectural awards. But somehow, it strikes me as overly pretty, lacking a clear statement of its structure. Gropius, I feel, would have done it differently."

"You see why I like her, Mac?" Colt asked. "Show me a girl with a fine mind, and I'm just sunk." Mac nodded in agreement. Unable to see Miss Smith's mind, he looked at the next best thing.

A few miles further on, we crossed the little bridge that joined City Island to the Bronx and went out Pilot Street. "Here we are," said Mac. Colt turned into a boatyard. A few big old hulls, propped up by timbers, were sitting on either side of the driveway, but most of the yard was empty. We parked and went out on the dock, hauling baggage and
food with us. On the way out, Mac said, "There she is, boys." We thought he meant the power boat moored to the float. "She looks roomy enough for a half-dozen or so," I said.

"Not there, sonny. Over there." He pointed over to one side of the dock. A small cabin sloop pulled up out of the water was resting on a wooden cradle.

"That little sailboat!" said Colt. "Why, not more than two people could sleep in there!"

"Not the boat, sonny. Look!" We looked again. A young woman was slapping copper colored paint on the bottom of the boat. She was wearing a faded blue denim shirt and some of those short overall pants, which are referred to, so help me, as pedal pushers. Her hair was pretty well covered with a bandanna. A generous sprinkling of the bronze paint made the flesh and costume look gilded and festive. My first reaction was that I wouldn't touch her with a ten-foot pole. Then she turned to dip her brush, and I saw her face. A smear of bronze was across her nose and one cheek, making her look like a painted Indian who needed a second coat. I decided to touch her with a ten-foot pole.

"You mean the kid?" asked Colt.

"She's no kid," I volunteered. Even the camouflage didn't hide that the denim shirt was extraordinarily well-filled.

"Are you trying to tell us," I asked Mac, "that she's the girl Bascomb is looking for?"

"Wouldn't say that, sonny. For all I can tell from here, maybe she's bald. I'm just sayin' when I saw her, I got a feelin'."

"Wait here a second, girls," said Colt.

"Not me," Peggy said. If this is the sexiest girl in the United States, I want to see her up close."

We left Miss Smith on the dock with the baggage and joined the young lady under the boat. "Nice job," Colt said. She turned and looked at us. I still wasn't convinced, but up close I could see that her eyes were big, dark, and sultry. Bedroom eyes, you might say, with a double bed. Under the copper bottom paint, her face was safe from barnacles and marine borers, but with her features, luscious and full-lipped and beautiful, she'd still be troubled with men.

The blue denim was smeared and dirty, but it was the best-shaped pair of overalls I ever saw. They were tight enough and soft enough to show off full, rounded breasts, a tiny waist, hips exactly ample enough, and legs that promised to be beautiful above the knees. You say you want more for your money? Step up a little closer, friend. That's close enough. She gave off a glow, like radiation, hitting you right between the legs.

One girl in umpteen million has it. Remember Jean Harlow? She had it. At least she did on the screen. When I was a kid, I saw all her pictures three times. She had a look of sheer, naked sex, lusty and voluptuous, sure, but mixed too with a dash of something like arrogance and maybe even cruelty. For my money, it had no more to do with love than Parcheesi. I wanted to rise out of my seat in the mezzanine and go for it. Well, this girl had it too.

"Yessir, sonny," said Mac softly,"! think this is the one." "

Are you the people," she asked, "who chartered the Sally Ann for the weekend?"

"Yep," said Mac. I was still tongue-tied.

"Power-boat men!" she said, shaking her head.

"What's wrong with power boats?" asked Colt.

"They oughtn't to allow 'em on the Sound," she said. She was kidding, partly but not entirely. "One of those big cruisers came plowing by at about twenty knots while we were filling up our water tank at the dock. Her waves threw us in so hard it crushed a plank."

"How would you like," asked Colt, "to have a sailboat like that one?" He pointed to a big, beautiful eight-meter sloop just heading into her mooring.

"No thanks," she said. "Have you ever tried to come up with a Genoa jib like that?"

"No," said Colt, who probably thought a genoa jib was some thing you served between antipasto and minestrone.

"If you don't catch it right, it pulls like a team of horses. You need a crew to sail that boat."

"How about that one?" asked Colt, pointing to a beautiful big cruising yawl lying at her mooring.

"Now you're talking. Two could handle her, and she's big enough to cruise in the open ocean. Say," she laughed, "if you're a yacht broker, don't look at our family. Too rich for our blood."

"Perhaps," said Colt, "we'll change all that." He introduced all of us, and she said her name was Lindsay. Gertrude Lindsay.

"Please," she added, "if this is a contest, I don't want to waste your time. My husband won't let me be in a contest."

"Your husband-?" I began stupidly.

"There he is," she said. "Coming down from the boatyard." He was a medium-sized, rather scholarly-looking man. He was almost bald, blond, wore glasses, had a round little paunch, and was about forty.

"It isn't a contest," said Colt. "Not exactly. If it is, I guess you already won. Have you ever been on the stage?"

"Not since high school. I was married very young." Her husband joined us. "Charles," she said, "these are the people that chartered the Sally Ann."

"Did you?" he asked. "I hope you'll pardon us. We want to finish this bottom. Like to get her in on this tide." He took the paintbrush from her. "I'll do the rest of this, dear. Would you mind checking with Olsen and finding out if he can put us over this evening?"

"All right," she said, wiping her hands on a rag. "I'll see you people later." She walked up toward the boatyard.

"Sonny," said Mac, "I'm goin' down to the boat and get things shipshape."

"I'll go with you," said Peggy, giving me a meaningful look. "I'll Be with you in a minute," I said.

"Mr. Lindsay," began Colt, "we represent an organization known as Electronics Research." Lindsay stopped his paintbrush in midstroke. "Gentlemen," he said, almost painfully, "I don't mean to be uncivil. But I warn you-—I'm beginning to develop a very nasty temper."

"But-" Colt started.

"Please. Just go away quietly. The last people who came out here to examine me went right off that dock."

"Examine you?" I exclaimed.

"We had to fish 'em out with a boat hook. And let me assure you, nothing new can be found. They've taken electro-cardio graphs, X-rays, blood counts, and urinalyses. They've tested my blood pressure, my hemoglobin, and my metabolism. I've been galvanometered, lie-detected, and psychoanalyzed. And I've willed my prostate to Harvard. Just go away, gentlemen, and leave my libido alone."

"All we want to do," said Colt, "is to make you rich."

"That," he said, "is the most indecent proposal I've ever heard in my life. By the latest count, I've fathered two hundred and thirty-seven healthy children by artificial insemination, but, I assure you, I haven't taken a cent in payment."

"Wait a minute," said Colt, "we're not talking about you." He put down the paintbrush and stared at us.

"You're not?"

"We're talking about your wife," I said.

"Well, you must understand that all this embarrasses her. She hadn't even realized, until the book came out, that there was anything unusual about us. And, of course, it was all my fault. I let the cat out of the bag before the book was published. Wild horses couldn't have dragged my name out of Dr. Kinsey."

"K-k-kinsey?" said Colt and I, in unison.

"Surely," he went on, "there are thousands of 'skilled and scholarly lawyers,' as he put it."

Dawn broke over Beecher. I remembered. I looked at him in open and honest admiration for a few seconds. A little guy, not much bigger than I was. And that round paunch and the balding head. He certainly didn't look sexy.

"You-you mean-" I stammered- "You? Thirty times a week?"

"Are you the hero of the Kinsey report?" asked Colt.

SEX MACHINE

He looked at us carefully for a minute as though he thought we were kidding him. "Didn't you know?"

"No," I replied. "Honestly."

"Well, then I beg your pardon, gentlemen. You can't imagine how I've been hounded."

"We came here," said Colt, "on a completely independent mission. We're conducting a survey to determine the—uh—most appealing woman in the United States. Or at least in these parts."

"She is a lovely girl, isn't she? My second wife. However, I have tried to keep her away from contests."

"It isn't a contest," said Colt. All we'd want to do is give Mrs. Lindsay a brief examination."

"You could be there," I added quickly.

"If she's the one we're looking for," Colt said, "neither of you will have to worry about money again."

"We don't worry about it now," he said. We lead very simple lives and spend a lot of time at home."

"Hobbies, I suppose?" I added, without thinking.

"No," he replied, "we don't seem to have much time for hobbies. Just sailing."

"Could mean a great deal, though," said Colt, still plugging. "An immediate contract for television, amounting to several hundred a week—expanding almost automatically as the number of sets increases. If she clicks, you could be quite wealthy."

"Some people might consider us quite wealthy right now," he said. "But perhaps you wouldn't understand that."

Colt did sort of a double take. He always had trouble under standing people interested in something other than money, but this case made a little more sense to him than most. "But just think," said Colt, "you'd be able to buy a boat like that." He pointed to the cruising yawl that Mrs. Lindsay had liked.

"Yes," he said. "Would be a temptation, alright."

"Come and see us, anyway," said Colt, giving him a card. So we waited a few minutes till Mrs. Lindsay came back. Not that we had to. We just wanted to, somehow. Then we walked out on the dock and boarded the Sally Ann, old but roomy. We met the young fellow, with crew-cut hair and faded Navy dungarees, who was going to run her for us.

As the sun sank in the west, we bade farewell to romantic City Island and the receding figures of the sexiest woman in the United States. Well, that was quite a weekend. We anchored in Lloyd's Harbor the first night and at Shelter Island on Saturday. Mac had plenty of time to fish, usually from the dinghy, where we wouldn't bother him. We had a lot of swimming in the daytime.

After the evening swim-that was Saturday we sat around on the fantail and had a few highballs. All but Mac. He went to bed early so he could get up to fish. We talked till after midnight, and it was all about Mac and the business. We wanted to get away from it, but we kept coming back.

"How much longer will it last?" Peggy asked.

"What do you mean?" Colt replied. "It ought to go on for years and years. Why not?" That was what we hoped, and of course, it could have happened. In fact, I don't think we realized, even then, just how far we could have gone and the tremendous power we could have wielded. But Colt wanted to grab every-thing we could, and I didn't make any real objections. After all, when you've never made more than sixty-five dollars a week in your life, you lose your bal-ance when more than a thousand dollars a week starts to roll in.

From here on, I'm getting to the part that you know. That everybody knows, I guess. You remember what happened to Mrs. Lindsay. Maybe not by that name. You know her as Lana Lindie, a name that Mac picked out of a list. We went through the formality of giving her a test on the machine, with Bascomb on hand, but under wraps. Mac gave her a rating of ninety-four, an all-time high.

"Geez, baby," said Bascomb, to everybody, "this is terrific!" And she was, too. Of course, she was out of the overalls and in a dress. Not particularly snaked up, you understand, the way she was later on, just normally clothed. But even Colt had to admit, when he saw her in nylons and high heels, that she had everything he could ask.

Bascomb signed her up, and to put her on display, he gave her a spot in his new television show. She didn't have to do much except look beautiful, smile, and give away refrigerators. And she did it so well that people took the refrig-erators whether they wanted them or not. It was about a month later, in early September, that she first went on the air over an East Coast CBS network. The very day of her premiere, we also signed a contract to put Slade on a nation-al hook-up. Bascomb was representing him on a split fee basis with us, and Portal's agency bought him for the West Coast to sell gasoline. Slade moved his headquarters to New York and brought Meacham with him. His total take, with beer in New England, gasoline on the West Coast, and a series of bakeries and soap flakes throughout the Midwest, all cut in simultaneously, came to more than three thousand dollars a week. Our share of this, siphoned off in three different ways, amounted to nearly a thousand.

"After ali," said Punchy, "there's a certain appeal in my voice quality. It's the confidential tone of a good friend. As a matter of fact, that's exactly what they said in Radio Guide."

"Did they?" Colt asked innocently, as though he hadn't seen the release before it left Bascomb's publicity writer. Punchy was sitting in our apartment with Meacham. Meacham still wore the black knit tie and still had a pasty look, but Punchy was in a brand-new gabardine by Brooks, and he must have been getting a fresh crew cut every four days. "It's a good thing we got out of Connecticut when we did," said Meacham. There was a lot of talk about running him for U.S. Senator."

"Well," I said, "you have to admit that the new story we worked out has got everything."We were campaigning for lower prices, higher wages, and more benefits to the farmer. It was perfect. It would do everything but work.

"It isn't that I'd mind being a Senator," said Punchy, "but do you know what they pay those fellows?" We didn't care about publicity for ourselves anymore. So of course, we began to get it. The Times gave us a front-page story as "a new toll in public opinion research," Written by their best scientific man. We let him see the machine but wouldn't let him examine it. This led to a slight note of skepticism in his story, but not appreciably more than appears in most of the Times articles on scientific discoveries.

The Times article started a flurry of statements in the press. Dr. Gallup told reporters he had never heard of us; the Hooper Company confirmed that Sladle had had a rapid rise in regional ratings but implied that while our system might assist in the analysis, it had very little relation to an overall compilation of program ratings. "It is difficult to see," their statement read, "how such a device could give computive , audience figures on programs broadcast simultaneously on four or more networks, together with the share of available audience regional breakdowns and sponsor identification figures." We had to admit to ourselves that they had a point.

Temple, my old boss at Standard-Idea, was not interviewed, but he did phone me.
"Congratulations, Fred. I didn't expect you'd do it. What's this electronic angle? I thought you said it was mental."

"You were right about that," I said, trying to think fast. "The mental part was just coincidence. This is scientific."

"Is it? Well, even if it isn't, Fred, you make them think it is."

"It really is," I protested. "You ought to see our machine."

"I'd like to."

"I'll give you a ring one of these days," I said. "Make your money while you can, Fred."

"What do you mean?"

"If you've really got what you say you've got, I'll give you six months." I puzzled over that for a long time, but I couldn't make anything out of it—not then. Now, as I look back, I think that Temple was the only man in the world who could see what was to happen.

But we were too busy to worry. After that first news story, there were articles by the dozen in all the trade papers, including Variety, Printers' Ink, Advertising Age, Tide, and Advertising and Selling. We had so many offers that we were dizzy. But most of them were from outfits competing with our clients' agencies, other package show producers, and other publishers. We told them no.

However, we could accept a few attractive propositions and one that almost blasted our company wide open. One acceptable deal came from the picture people. We had a few feelers from big companies, but most would have meant moving to the Coast. Then one of the new independent companies called us. You know, one of those outfits set up by a director and a couple of stars so that the money could come under capital gains instead of salary. Lower taxes. They were making a film in New York, one with a lot of local color. They offered us a fee of five thousand dollars.

"Five thousand?" sneered Colt. "We wouldn't touch it for that. We work only on a percentage basis. Say, twenty-five per cent of your net profit." They screamed. But they settled for fifteen percent, and we agreed to review their story in varying stages, from rough treatment to the final shooting script. We were to help cast all but the starring roles, look at "rushes," the day-to-day crop of rough cut film, at least twice a week, and select a title, an advertising slogan, layouts for their principal posters and advertisements.

Another offer we could accept came a few weeks later from Everybody's Own Magazine, the new slick paper monthly that was beginning to worry Cosmopolitan, the Ladies Home Journal, and the American. Colt and I went to see the editor, Mrs. Lydia Maple. She had an ultra-modern office with partitions of glass brick. Everything in it was scaled down, including her tiny kidney-shaped desk to make Mrs. Maple seem larger.

She was about five feet tall and seemed to be under Forty, though her prematurely white hair was tinted almost lavender.

"Read about you men. Cigarette? Is it really true? I certainly] hope so. They're doing it now, you know, research in the magazines. Redbook's done it for years, and others too. We've done ii, had to. Surveyed what we call 'signals.' Know what a signal is? Tota! impact of the layout of the story. You know, title, illustration, caption, subtitle. find what percentage will be hooked into reading it. Hell of a difference. Some rate three times the others. Nothing to do with the writing of the story, understand. Just the signal. So far, most surveys have been made after the magazine is all printed. After the horse is out of the barn. Gives you an idea of what to buy and how to lay out the signals, maybe two issues ahead. You can do better—can't you?"

The machine-gun chatter stopped abruptly. She ground out a cigarette and looked from one to the other of us very quickly, turning her head instantly, bing-bing, the way a bird does. "Yes," said Colt, "we'll eliminate guesswork. We'll react to story synopses, rough illustrations, ten different titles, subtitles, and captions."

"How much?" she asked, the way they all did.

Colt made a deal, as we'd agreed, for immediate cash-fifteen hundred dollars a month for the first six months. She gave us a check for the first fifteen hundred before we left her office.

PULP CULTURE PRESS

CHAPTER ELEVEN

Meantime, as the work piled up, we tried to make every thing as painless as possible for Mac. He didn't have to sit at the machine, of course, except as window dressing for a client. We often brought layouts, scripts, or magazine stories to his apartment. And there was that beautiful September afternoon when we hired a big rowboat on Great South Bay.

"Man the oars," Peggy ordered. "Today, you boys are galley slaves."

"I'm a man of wealth," said Colt. I can rent you a steam yacht or buy you an outboard motor."

"Uncle Mac doesn't like outboard motors," said Peggy. "Scares the fish, sonny."

"Stroke!" said Peggy. "Twenty to the minute will be fast enough."

And so we blistered our hands under the hot September sun while Mac and Peggy stretched at their ease, like Antony and Cleopatra on a barge. Mac fished happily while Peggy asked him questions. The results were the same, we supposed, as Mac could have given us anywhere. But we had one hell of a time explaining the fish scales on those layouts.

The magazine surveys seemed to be moving along satisfactorily. It was the newspaper proposition that nearly split our company in two. That happened about a month later, in October. We were just getting ready to move the machine to our new offices, in rooms adjoining Portal's agency. He had found some space in a Park Avenue building that was initially a swank apartment hotel. But we were still in the brownstone when Tindale called. It was a Thursday afternoon. Mac came over after dinner, and we were getting things in shape. Peggy, by then a full-time employee, was helping me sort and simplify the material we would present to Mac. Colt was sitting behind a temporary partition, dictating to Diana and looking at her legs. (You remember Diana from my old office at Standard-Idea. I'd recommended her when it was obvious we needed secretarial help, and Colt had approved her enthusiastically after studying her qualifications from the navel down.)

As I say, we were all there when Tindale arrived. He had made an appointment, and he was right on time. He was tall and blond, with a long, thin, aristocratic face.

"I'm mighty glad to meet you," he said and sat down. He was very expensively but somehow loosely dressed, in a soft oxford shirt and generously cut flannel suit that fit him like a bathrobe. The commodore," he said, "is very interested in your gadget.

SEX MACHINE

He'd like exclusive newspaper rights for all his papers."

He meant, of course, Commodore Briskley's chain of newspapers, more than a dozen of them, scattered over the whole country. They were mostly tabloid in size and flamboyant in illustrations, typography, and colored inks. They reflected, not only in their editorials but in news stories and four-color cartoons on page one, the strange anachronistic mind of Commodore Briskley. He was a medieval knight in shining armor, riding a white elephant, and on his shield was a screaming American eagle. He was a nationalist, an isolationist, a paternal ist, a tory, a feudal lord, and a master at throwing dust in the eyes of the people. In some cities, his papers were waning slightly in popularity, but generally, they still held first place in circulation.

Peggy looked at Tindale, relaxed in the chair, his eyes partly closed. "I didn't know," she said, "that the commodore cared what people thought. Tindale didn't even move his drooping eyelids.

"Oh, but the commodore does care what people think. He's a very firm believer in democracy, the commodore is."

Colt said quickly, "We can always tell you exactly what people want." Tindale made me feel a little queasy in my stomach. I am still trying to figure out why. Somehow, he seemed partly decomposed without being completely dead. "Why does he care what people think," I asked, "if he's going to tell them how to think?"

"In a few cities," said Tindale, "our circulation is slipping. The commodore and I think you could help, mostly with the frosting. Comics, for instance. Of course, we survey them now, but we thought you might give us an idea of the advance plot. The same goes for columns, departments, contests, and all that."

"We could do it," said Colt, "but it would take a lot of time."

"It should be worthwhile," said Tindale. "Whatever anyone is paying you, the commodore will pay you more." Colt smiled happily. "Take this fellow, Slade," Tindale continued. "What you did for him, you could do for us. Even in our news columns. Certainly in our editorials. With one rather important exception, of course. I imagine you tell Slade what to say. Just make it popular. Just get a rating. With us, we'll tell you what to say, and you'll tell us how to say it. Big difference. Give them their reasons for doing what we want. Think about it for a minute. Might make us and you with us, of course rather important force."

I stood up, swaying slightly. "Just a minute," I said, rather stupidly. I wanted to say something sharp, like, "My mother didn't raise her son to be a putty knife." I never think of lines like that till afterward. "Just a minute, Mr. Tindale," I repeated.

"Yes?" asked Tindale, moving just one side of his mouth and eyeballs.

Colt jumped up. "I think Mr. Tindale and I had better straighten out the financial side of things first."

Tindale looked at his nails. "The commodore has been rais ng his prices for years to compensate people for their ideals. However, there is a limit."

"I think you'd better go," I said. I could just see Beecher marching along with a fife, drum, and bloody bandages.

"Conversely," said Tindale, "if things work out, the money might come pretty high. Maybe as high as a million dollars."

"A million?" asked Colt in a reverent voice.

"Or more. Who knows? Depends on how much money you make for us."

A million dollars. I almost sat down. I even started to rationalize, the way people do when the ante is raised too close to the asking price of an Ideal, which of course, is priceless. You don't say, "Well, for that price I'll have to sell!" You try to say, "After all, is it so bad? What real harm can it do?"

I'd like to pretend it happened this way. He (Beecher) stood there quietly. He felt he could hear the distant clamor of a fife and drum. Slowly, he reached into his pocket and drew out a five-cent piece. He read the words E Pluribus Unum, inscribed beside the walls of Monticello. He turned the coin and looked at the face of Tom Jefferson. His young lips were set in a firm line, and a fire was burning in his eyes. "Go!" he said. Tindale trembled, turned white, and left without a word. Didn't work like that, though.

In the first place, my little mental slide rule kept saying, "With what you're going to be making, boy, you'll keep damned little of that million." And I could see Peggy standing up, too. I knew if I didn't sound off, she would I said, "I don't think we're interested, Mr. Tindale."

"Wait a minute," said Colt.

"You don't have to make up your minds now," said Tindale, without trembling or turning white. He stood up and turned to the door.

"Beecher doesn't mean that!" said Colt.

"Yes, he does!" said Peggy.

"I do, too!" I said heroically.

"Well," said Tindale, out of the corner of his mouth, "it's been a real pleasure meeting you people. You know where to reach me." And he sauntered out.

Colt swung around at us. "Maybe," he began, in a too-steady voice, like a short fuse, already lit, "maybe you didn't hear what he said. A million bucks!"

"I heard him," I said.

"I heard him, too," said Peggy.

"Maybe," Colt repeated, the fuse getting shorter, "maybe you thought it was good strategy to put him off like this. Raise the price, huh?"

"No," I said. Peggy shook her head in the same direction. "I'll be god-damned!" Colt exploded. "Throwing a million bucks in the gutter! I'm going right down to see him tomorrow morning!

"If you do," said Peggy, "I'll go straight to Uncle Mac."

"Me, too!" I said bravely.

"Who needs Mac?" he screamed. "You sure picked one hell of a time to start growing a set of ideals!" He spun around, walked out, and slammed the door. Let's see. About three weeks later, we moved into our new offices. And what a three weeks! Maybe it's lucky we were so busy-no time to fight. After Colt simmered down, we returned to work and tried to forget about the commodore.

One morning, about ten days after the commodore incident, Peggy reported for work at her usual time, around nine-thirty. Diana was already on hand, typing away at the speed of light, and the two of us, informally draped in slacks and moccasins, were lapping sleepily at cups of coffee. "Look at this," said Peggy, showing us her morning paper. "Harry Grope took a swing at us this morning." Harry Grope was a forthright radio columnist who used a minimum of press-agent releases.

Grope had seen the latest ratings, and he knew about us, too. He commented on Slade, who was rising into the top fifteen programs on the air, and on another commentator who had the misfortune to be opposite him on another network simultaneously. The other fellow, MacLean, had just been canceled by his sponsor. "MacLean," wrote Grope, "made the unpardonable error of telling his listeners what he believed to be the truth, even when the truth was unpleasant and unpopular. Slade, on the other hand, is a vacuum, which may be abhorred by nature but not by the listening public. They rushed in, so to speak, to fill the vacuum, and the effect was something like a thunder clap.

"It may seem to you at first that the error is with the public, but I question whether it's the function of the public to write scripts for Mr. Slade. It's a silly idea that a commentator, like a writer or statesman or any other alleged leader, should be walking a few paces out front. Not that the people should not exercise some control over him, for they should. But it strikes me that if nobody is going to lead, we won't go anyplace unless it's around in circles.

"Of course you may say, so long with Mrs. Grope that you don t want to go anywhere.

"To me," said Colt, "that sounds like nonsense."

"Look down here," said Peggy. "See what he says about the Gasoline Hour." That was Portal's variety show, music, and comedy, which was rising rapidly in rating. "I have noticed one frightening thing about this program," wrote Grope, "apart from the fact that such comparative tripe should be so popular. It appears to be setting a pretty rigid pattern, too. Not only does it seem to be imitating itself from week to week, but already other programs are be ginning to imitate it." Grope cited several new programs which were certainly imitations of ours.

"As I write this," Grope continued, "little groups of well tailored young men are sitting around the offices of advertising agencies and program package producers, thinking how closely they can duplicate the Gasoline Hour without giving grounds for legal action.

"It seems to me that a certain kind of rigidity is beginning. Almost, you might say, a sort of rigor mortis. Where it will end, I hesitate to say."

There was a bit of talk about the Grope column, but nothing happened. Portal was slightly concerned but not worried, and, as far as I know, the client never heard about it. And when you're as busy as we were, you don't fret much. That very evening "New York's first sex riot" occurred, to quote the tabloid papers. Miss Lana Lindie (Mrs. Charles Lindsay (having graduated from refrigerator-giving had the premiere of her first actual television program. All she did was half talk and half sing and look like she wanted to take the camera to bed with her. The effect was cataclysmic. Great crowds, distinctly not bobby-soxers, converged on the studio. The attack was spearheaded by hirelings from Bascomb's publicity depart ment, but they amounted to little more than the yeast in the dough. Thousands came from bar and grills, and bistros in the Radio City area.

Like so much bullion, Miss Lindie finally had to be removed in an armored car like a mound of bouillon, happily imprisoned by Bascomb's head publicity man. The next day Miss Lindie had a five-year picture contract, beginning at twenty-five hundred dollars a week.

"Geez, baby," shouted Bascomb over the phone, "it's a regular coop we pulled. The first movie contract in history specifies she can keep on with her TeeVee program-and shoot all her movies in New York!" There were even predictions by Mayor O'Dwyer that the reign of Hollywood had ended. Charles Lindsay's only comment was, "I'll never forgive you as long as I live! I'd sue the pants off of you if I knew what to sue you about!"

SEX MACHINE

The same week, Manners House also heard from Hollywood. "Rather good luck," Manners said. "Offered us a hundred thousand, and the book isn't even finished. Just based on the synopsis and a dozen chapters." We were already making preliminary surveys for a second book.

"I don't like to complain," he said when I mentioned the other job, "but it's beginning to shape up pretty much like number one. Sometimes, it's a bit hard to tell them apart. Not that I consider it a complete disadvantage. We'll have a new title, of course, and a different dust jacket. It does worry me, though." It was beginning to worry me, too.

Meanwhile, we were cooking on several other burners. Our independent movie company was rapidly reaching the shooting script stage. Based on the early "treatments," the writer-director was impressed.

He was a tall, gaunt man who looked like Abraham Lincoln. He said, "Freddie, we will have the most popular picture ever produced. It will be a treasure house of heartthrobs and gentle laughter. And sex. It is a man's picture, yes, but mostly it is a woman's picture. Freddie, after seeing this picture, they won't have a natural emotion for days. They will be washed out, wrung out, and hung up to dry. The effect will be the same as a good enema. Mrs. Maple, too, seemed to be pleased.

"Excellent. Really excellent," she said over the phone. "Signal in this issue are going to be powerful. illustrations, caption, everything. Irresistible. Don't see how they will put the book down once they open it. One thing, though. Just one worry. Last set of results."

"Not good?"

"Excellent. But a wee bit similar to the others. What happens if we finally achieve perfection? Will every issue be exactly alike?" None of these things bothered Colt. The money was rolling in, and that was all he asked. We bought a big television set that we almost had to climb over it to get into the apartment. And Colt traded in his Chevy for a Lincoln convertible, about the size of a B-29. And then, of course, there was the new apartment. "I just bought an apartment," he said when he came home one afternoon.

"You bought it? A whole building?"

"No. It might have been cheaper, though. One of those new co-ops. You buy the place, two thousand down, then you pay off the mortgage and the maintenance. That's the only way you can get one now. East Seventy-sixth Street. It has a huge living room, with a terrace and a bar, two bedrooms, and two bathrooms."

"Did I buy it, too?"

"You can live there, Beech, till you and Peggy build your house. It isn't finished yet, though. We can't move in for more than a month."

As for me, I was saving my money. Peggy and I had bought a lot up in Westchester, near those pine forests and the Kensico reservoir. We had an architect working on plans for a solar house, of red brick and cyprus. "I don't know," said Peggy, "it seems like a strange thing to build a house on, this whole business, I mean. Kind of like building it on a swamp."

"It worries me, too," I said. But then we'd look at the straight, clean lines of the architect's drawings, and I'd look at the round, clean lines of Peggy Maddox, and for quite awhile we wouldn't care whether democracy was pure or not. As far as we could tell, Mac didn't change a bit, not even his brand of tobacco or the way he rolled his cigarettes.

"What do you do with your money, Mac?" Colt asked him.

"Bought me a fishin' boat, sonny."

"What are you saving for?"

"A shack in the woods, sonny."

"You could buy a hundred of 'em right now," Colt said.

"Figure of speech, boy, I'll take my simplicity piped in, like I told Freddie here. Few more months like this, and I'll be able to pipe it in for life."

"A few more months!" Colt screamed.

"You don't figure this is gonna last, do you, Sonny?" He looked at us out of the corner of his eye, hunched over the Gimmick like a buzzard over a dead dog. The Gimmick sat on the inlaid floor, like a robot on a chaise lounge.

"Boy, look at all the room!" shouted Colt, swinging his arms. Portal was standing beside us, pale, tight-lipped, and outwardly very calm and quiet.

"Your own offices are in the next room," he said, leading us out of what must have been the living room into a bedroom that had been partitioned into two spacious offices, each one having a large window, a big shiny desk, easy chairs, and a couch. There was another room for typists, with three desks. "It was formerly a kitchen," Portal added. "All the equipment was taken out."

"What do you know!" said Colt. "A bathroom!"

"We have twelve bathrooms in our offices," said Portal "Didn't seem to be able to convert them." We went to Portal's offices, which occupied the entire floor above. His own office must have been a former master bedroom, in a corner with four windows. "Sit down, gentlemen," he said softly. He explained our official opening, which was to be the following day. His publicity department had arranged for reporters.

"Is that really necessary?" I asked.

"No, but it will be precious publicity for the agency. We've absorbed all our current accounts very well, and we're anxious to attract new business. Do you have any objections?"

"Well-" I began, not knowing how to explain that the Gimmick wouldn't stand up under scientific inspection.

"No objection," said Colt quickly. He told me later he was thinking the same thing, but didn't know what to do about it.

"Very well, gentlemen." Portal pressed one of several buttons on his desk phone, picked it up, and said, "Is Mr. Munson waiting outside? . . . Have him come in, please." He turned to us. "Mr. Munson is from the Hooper service. I arranged to have your appointments together. He said he had something very strange to tell me, and he was afraid to say it over the phone."

Mr. Munson came in, a dapper, nervous little man with white hair, a white mustache, and a florid complexion. "Gentlemen," he said after the introductions, "I have a most curious phenomenon to report to you. One of the most curious in the entire history of audience research. When our telephone survey people first reported it, I hesitated to believe it. Then, during your last broadcast, I took over some of the calls personally, and I can tell you—it's true."

"The Gasoline Hour?" Portal asked.

Munson nodded. "As you know, we make our calls during the time the program is on the air. We ring a number of times. Our national average is in the neighborhood of 3.4 rings before the instrument is picked up- if the party is at home. Now, during the Gasoline Hour, this figure rose to 5.8!"

"Five point eight?" I repeated foolishly.

"Five point eight five, actually. We could say five point nine."

"Go on," said Portal.

"More than that, gentlemen. The party answering the phone often sounded as though he or she had been awakened from a sound sleep. I have here a transcript of one typical interview. I'll read it. "Were you listening to your radio just now?' 'Hello. Mmmmmm? Whozzat?' 'Were you listening to your radio just now?' 'Must have been asleep. Whazzat again?' 'Were you listening to your radio just now?' 'Mmmmmm. Yeah. It's on. Sure.' 'To what program were you listening, please?' 'Oh. Lemme see. Oh, yeah. Gasoline Hour.' 'What is advertised?' 'Oh, gasoline, I guess.' 'What brand of gasoline?' 'Couldn't say, brother. Guess I musta been asleep.' "

"Perhaps that accounts for the fact that our sponsor identification figure has been dropping," said Portal.

"It's very peculiar," said Munson. "Some of the people interviewed volunteered information like this. 'Best little program on the air, yessir. Always tune it in. Just can't seem to stay awake, is all.'"

A few moments later, Munson left. "I can't understand it," said Colt.

Portal sat quietly for a while. Then he spoke, almost in a whisper. "I can make a guess. You don't have children, do you, gentlemen?" We shook our heads. "Every advertising man should. People are so much like them. Ask a child what story he wants to hear, and of course, he'll say, 'The Three Bears' or some other story he's already heard. After all, how can he ask for a story he has never heard? Then, as you tell it, he'll drop off contentedly to sleep."

"What can we do about it?" I asked.

"Nothing, gentlemen. Soon, we'll have all the top-ranking programs on the air, which alone will be enough to provide us with more clients than we can handle. Our system of research is, not at fault. We're simply doing what everyone else is doing, only doing it more efficiently.

"Perhaps, if our audience is asleep, we will have to study the best way to instill desires in the sleeping mind. Repetition, I believe, has been found successful. Perhaps 'Air Line Gasoline is fine gasoline. Yes, Air Line Gasoline is fine gasoline. Get Air Line Gasoline, the fine gasoline today!' Who knows? As a form of mass hypnosis, it may be quite effective.

"I'll see you, gentlemen, then, tomorrow at your grand opening." And as we walked out, I could hear those voices. In a singsong chant, they seemed to be repeating, "Pure democracy is fine democracy. Yes, pure democracy is fine democracy. Get pure democracy—today!"

CHAPTER TWELVE

And now, gentlemen," said Colt, "we'll give you a demonstration of the Psychoelectronic Correlator." Outside the sun was shining brightly, and long strips of golden light lay on the floor, the way they will in November when the sun is low. I point that out because it has an important bearing on the disaster that was to follow.

As usual, Mac was bent over the machine, but he was all out of character with a fresh shave, haircut, and newly pressed suit. Portal and his publicity men were there, and about a dozen reporters. They were seated in a row about ten feet from the Gimmick. I might add that we'd had a huge cabinet built around the machinery. It made visible a maximum of flashing lights, knobs, spark-gaps, and other gimcracks but disguised its real identity.

"Perhaps," said Colt, "you have some sample questions of your own that we could put to the machine."

"Yes, I have one," said a middle-aged woman with a face like a woodchuck and a scratchy voice. I didn't know it then, but I soon discovered that she was Bettina Kleagle, a Commodore Briskley's New York tabloid feature writer. "We made our own survey," continued Miss Kleagle. "We asked how many people approved of the administration's policy toward Russia. We haven't yet published those figures. No one in this room knows them but me. Can you duplicate them?"

"Just a moment," I said. "We can find out what opinions are now—and that may differ somewhat from the opinions you gathered a week or more ago."

"I'll take that chance," said Kleagle.

"All right," said Colt, "just step to this microphone and give us your question." The bands of sunlight on the floor were moving slowly. Already one of them touched the machine. I remember an impulse to turn the blinds, but for some reason I didn't obey it. Kleagle stepped up and read her question. Mac pushed the button. I saw where it stopped and read out a figure.

Out of the corner of my eye, I noticed that the fluorescent lighting in the ceiling had gone off. I wouldn't have noticed if I hadn't seen the actual tubes. As I said, the sunlight was pouring in, and we didn't need any light. It didn't occur to me then that if no one had pulled the cord on the lighting fixture, it couldn't have gone out unless something had happened to the power. Kleagle read another question, and Mac pushed the button. I announced the figure. We repeated this process half a dozen times.

"Well," said Colt, when she had finished, "how did we do?"

SEX MACHINE

"Beautifully," rasped Miss Kleagle. "Your results are almost identical to ours." She read our figures and hers. They were quite close, most of them within about one percent. There was a murmur of approval. The reporters seemed quite impressed.

"May I ask you just two more questions?" said Kleagle.

"Of course," Colt replied.

"Your machine operates electronically, doesn't it? In other words, without electricity it would be powerless?"

"Of course," Colt repeated.

"May I ask your operator whether he noted any difference in the machine's efficiency between question number one and question number two?"

We all looked at Mac. "No, ma'am." Mac, still bent over but turning his head, "didn't notice a thing." For the first time, I saw that the lights in the machine were all out. Even if they'd been on, there would have been only a faint glow so bright was the sunlight. Then, of course, I remembered the ceiling light.

"I accuse you," said Miss Kleagle, "of perpetrating a gigantic swindle and hoax. Since the first question, there hasn't been one volt of electricity in that dingbat. I know. I had a man out in the hall at the fuse box."

"Out of my way!" shouted one reporter, running for the door. Portal stood up. I'd never seen such a look of horror on his deadpan features.

"Wait a minute!" screamed Colt.

"If you need any further proof," said Kleagle, "I call your attention to that electric clock." It was a nice new one. We'd just bought it. "It stopped exactly eight minutes ago." Several more reporters were already out the door.

"I can explain it!" Colt was yelling. "The auxiliary power—I mean the batter-ies, I mean—" Mac was on his feet, facing the reporters. He put a hand on Colt's shoulder. "You're makin' it worse, sonny," he said. He wasn't excited. He didn't even seem to care. "I think maybe we better tell 'em the truth."

Mac affected the crowd like a shot of morphine. For a few seconds, there wasn't a sound. Then a reporter said, "You admit the gadget is a fake?"

"Yes, it is, sonny. The boys got it off a battleship, didn't you?"

"Yes," I said weakly.

"See," Mac went on, "they figured that these days nobody believes in anything but gadgets. Maybe they're right. They figured if they set me up as some kind of a swami, everybody'd just laugh. Probably would have, too. Yessir, the lights and gimcracks there are phony as all get out. But there's nothin' phony about MacInnes."

"How do you spell that?" asked a reporter. Mac spelled it out.

"Don't care for myself," said Mac. "I can take this business or leave it alone. But these are nice boys and I don't think they aimed to cheat anybody. Maybe you better tell 'em how this all got started, boys."

We told it all, Colt and I. I had to start because Colt was groggy and dazed. We started right at the beginning, when I was at Standard Idea, and we put in plenty of facts and exact figures.

"You can check those," I said.

"And put down, too," added Colt, "that Macinnes hasn't been proved wrong yet."

"Doesn't mean," said Mac, "that I can't be. Don't guarantee a thing."

Finally the last reporter left. The last one was Miss Kleagle. "I still think," she said, "that it's a phony."

"Thanks for everything," said Colt sourly. We were alone with Portal.

"You won't need all this office space, will you?" he said.

"We'll have to take out the machine," said Colt.

"You may have to take out everything. Gentlemen, I don't much care whether you're mechanical or mental, but I do mind your not telling me."

There wasn't anything to say. Finally, Portal shrugged his shoulders. "I'm going to talk to our clients now, so that they'll hear it from us before the stories break.' Not long after that we walked out sadly, wondering whether we'd reached the bottom of the gold mine of Macinnes.

We made page one of every afternoon paper in New York, and most of them had a two—or three-column headline. Some of them were tough and uncompromising: ELECTRONIC POLL MACHINE A FAKE, OWNERS ADMIT, that sort of thing. ELECTRONIC HOOPER A PHONY.

The World-Telegram had their funniest feature writer do a story that they illustrated with a cartoon. IT'S ALL A BRAIN WAVE, SAY INSTANT RESEARCHERS the headline read. Of the morning papers, Colonel Briskley's tabloid was the

SEX MACHINE

most savage, with a signed expose by Bettina Kleagle. HOW I EXPOSED THE ELECTRONIC POLL

.

The Times gave a studious report headlined RESEARCHERS ASSERT MENTAL ASPECT OF SURVEY FAILS TO AFFECT ACCURACY.

However, a great many things happened between the afternoon and the morning papers. We retreated temporarily to our apartment and tried to reach all our clients before they heard the news elsewhere. We talked to Punchy Slade first.

"What I mean is, we do it mentally, Punchy."

"Yes? That's good, isn't it, Fred?"

"The machine was just window dressing."

"What machine? That big thing in your living room? I never did understand that, Fred. Don't you use it anymore?"

"No. It's all in Mac's mind." "

Changed, huh?"

"No, we always did it that way. Shouldn't affect your ratings, Punchy."

"Oh, fine then."

"Put Meacham on, will you?"

I gave Meacham all our side of the story, and he agreed to include it for almost fifteen minutes in the script that evening. It was a real human story, be-ginning with the ancient prophets and ending with Macinnes, the modern seer. Of course, Slade, the omniscient, had known it all along, but he was afraid no one would believe it. Slade read it on the air just that way.

Manners was delighted. "Keep it mental, by all means, boys. I much prefer it to machinery. One thing, though. If it is in the old fellow's head, can't he throw my writers a few curves? Second book is beginning to look like a carbon copy of the first one!"

Mrs. Maple was concerned about her advertisers, but primarily she was excit-ed. "Promise me his story. I'll send a writer there tomorrow. Squeeze it into the January issue, I can make the January one if I throw out the-—yes, I can."

The movie, people didn't mind-but their bankers did, after they saw the newspapers. They didn't trust anything mental. It looked like they were going to junk the whole script and dhree Musketeers.

Portal called us in the late afternoon. The gasoline people had canceled the account.

An hour later, he called again. The widow of the manufacturer of an under-arm deodorant had phoned him. She was a spiritualist and an astrologer, and she spent two million dollars a year in magazines, radio, and newspapers, telling people about their armpits. She was extremely interested in Macinnes, and, therefore in the Portal agency.

But it was Bascomb who really surprised us. He was so busy we couldn't reach him until after the first papers hit the stands. "Geez, baby, it's terrific! I'm sending over a contract now, my boy!"

"Contract for what?"

"The old geezer, who else, baby? I want to sign him up. Just the agent's fees are all. Ten percent. I can pick up a quick thousand this week on 'We the People,' and that's radio and TeeVee both. Maybe we can make him up so he doesn't look three days dead. We'll keep a recording and a teletranscription of the show. Then we'll sell him with his own program. I'm workin' out the gimmick now."

"Please. Just don't use that word."

"Okay, baby, but the old guy's a natural. How do you like 'The Certified Amateur Hour.' First, the old boy picks 'em out, maybe the top five or six performers, see, before the broadcast. Sure, he knows from the start which one is tops, but we keep 'em guessing. Which one gets the orchids or whatever the gimmick is. Sorry, baby, I mean, whatever the routine is, we work out. He's right on the show, see, Mac is, and maybe he's even got on a towel around the head; you know, a turban, for the camera, if it's video too."

"I don't think Mac would wear a turban."

"Okay, so it's a crystal ball or a magic wand, maybe. Just so it's visual. This is a new medium, baby, and we gotta think about the visual. But the big dough is still the regular radio broadcast. Can the old boy talk?"

"He can, I think, but I'm not sure that he will."

"He will when he sees what kind of lettuce there is in this deal. I betcha we can get five a week for the package with his publicity."

"Five hundred?"

"Five thousand, baby. And what are your costs? Script, a couple hundred; an emcee, maybe five more; and music, about a thousand or under. The amateurs—hell, they'll fall all over themselves to get on for nothing, and you pick up extra on them anyway with commissions on the traveling units. The whole deal is natural, and, of course, you and Fleming are in on the package. Whatta you say, baby?"

"I'll have to talk to Mac," I said.

Naturally, Colt became very excited about Bascomb's idea. "I think it'll work," he said. "You get enough publicity and you can parlay it into anything." Mac was less enthusiastic.

"I dunno, sonny. I've got a funny feeling the whole thing's not gonna last."

"Well," said Colt, "maybe that's all the more reason we should make a killing while we can."

"And besides," I added, "if you like to be nice and warm, Mac, you'll be the happiest man in television. They broil you alive."

"I'll do it, sonny," said Mac, "but I got the most peculiar feelin' I ever had. It's kinda like you're on a roly-coaster and you're goin' down a hill. And no matter what you do, you can't stop it, and you can't get out."

"I'll do it, sure-but it's not gonna last."

During that week, we had coverage about equal to a World Series or a Presidential election. There were pictures and stories in all the papers. There were newsreels, an article in Life, and a cover on Time. Mac was on "We the People" and was interviewed by Mary Margaret McBride.

He was investigated by the Society for Psychic Research and the Better Business Bureau. Duke University sent a delegation to play those card tricks with him and test him for extrasensory perception. He had it, but then (they say), so do you, and you. His score at guessing cards he couldn't see was much better than the law of averages said it should be. Then they tested me, and my score was ten percent higher than Mac's.

What this proves, I wouldn't know. We also had offers from both Republican and Democratic National Committees. We shelved them for the time being. And there was that group out in Los Angeles, too. They called themselves The Great We Know, and they appointed Mac a sort of God Almighty, with jurisdiction extending, no doubt, to the Los Angeles city limits. As far as we could tell, the main organizers were a couple of unemployed promoters and a minor-league evangelist. The victims were drawn partly from the old Angelus Temple crowd and from assorted cults and old-age pension groups. They had their headquarters and temporary temple in an abandoned supermarket. They immediately published plans for a glass-brick and stucco tabernacle, with a statue of MacInnes seventy-five feet high. Colt started to suit against them. "I don't care," he said. If they want, they can even declare Jackson Heights a Holy City—just as long as they give us a cut."

All Mac did was shake his head. It's not going to last, Sonny. I've got a terrible feeling it's not gonna last."

Peggy was there one time when he said that. "Why do you think it won't last, Uncle Mac?"

"Don't know, kiddy, but every now and then, I get kind of a muddy feeling,"

"Muddy?"

"Things don't come over so clear. You take the other day when I was on that program, that 'We the People.' Now if you'd have asked me right then, when I was on the air, to give you a reaction on somethin', I couldn't have done it."

"Maybe you were just excited," I said.

"I was fussed up, sonny, sure. But you know, I figured it was more than that. Ten million people were thinkin' about me. It kinda swarmed in on me, all those people thinkin' about me, and everything went blank for a minute. I don't know. Sort of a big backwash, maybe, floodin' in and drownin' out every thing else. After the show was over, it got better, but every day now, it seems to build up a little more.

"And that's not all, sonny. I've been talkin' to people. Like Manners and that Maple girl. And I've been thinkin'. You know, I'm just beginning to catch on to what we're doin' to the whole country.

"Maybe the country's just tryin' to hit back."

And when Peggy and I were alone, she said, "Fred, don't you think it's time we stopped?"

"I have here," I said, "an estimate from the contractor. The architect seems to have been optimistic. By about seventy-five hundred dollars. Or maybe you'd rather not build the house."

"That's a terrible decision to have to make."

"Who knows—maybe we won't have to make it."

Well, maybe I'm not psychic (even though Duke University isn't entirely sure), but that's exactly how things happened. We never did have to decide... Bascomb did put the Certified Amateur Hour together, and he sold it in record time to our lady of the armpits. She gave her account of Portal, who made an ingenious deal with us. We were to receive a basic thirty-five hundred a week for the show, plus a raise of five hundred a week for every point we rose in rating.

"Geez, baby," said Bascomb, "if this goes like I think it'll go, we'll be knocking off ten grand a week inside of twenty-six weeks!"

Since the No-Swette people already owned the air time, we were able to start the program in just three weeks. Portal simply had to cancel the show currently filling the half-hour, a surprisingly intelligent documentary. It was building a loyal audience—but not quite rapidly enough. We bought television time, too, on a network covering the whole East Coast. Both the broad cast and the telecast would be done simultaneously.

And so it was that we had the great history-making MacInnes broadcast, the most famous one since the Martian invasion. There was every reason to suspect things would go the way they did, but we wouldn't believe it. In the first place, during the week before the broadcast Mac refused to make any surveys.

"Why not?" asked Colt.

"You just wait, sonny. Wait till after that radio show." In the amateur auditions, he picked a string quartet. Out of twenty-five acts trying out, Mac was supposed to pick the six that would have the most popular appeal, and on the air, he was supposed to give the grand prize to one of them.

"Are you sure, baby?" asked Bascomb.

Mac nodded. He had picked four other acts; a ventriloquist, some rhythm singers, an impersanator, and a comedian-pretty standard stuff, and nobody disagreed.

"But a stringed quartet, baby!"

"Isn't it a good quartet? I thought they played mighty pretty."

"Sure, they played okay, and maybe they'd lay 'em in the aisles in Town Hall, but this is radio, baby! On this kind of a show, a stringed quartet is deader than a mackerel! The only way they got in was somebody thought it was a barbershop quartet."

"It isn't up to me," said Mac. "It's up to them."

"They liked 'em, huh?" Mac nodded again.

Bascomb shook his head. "Okay. I'll go along with it. But geez, a stringed quartet!"

That wasn't all. During that last week, I noticed something peculiar about Mac. It was so vague and l so subtle that I just sensed it more than anything else. Mac had always been gentle and considerate, but now he was not only kinder and gentler to us, but he was also in a strange way more solicitous, more anxious to please, and obviously more careful not to offend. I remember one little episode during a rehearsal when I asked him some question.

"Oh, run along, sonny, don't you see I'm busy!" But he had that twinkle in his eyes, and I knew he was fooling.

"Oh, sorry, Mac," I said. Then he looked back at me twice, trying to see whether I knew he was just joking.

"I'm just kiddin', sonny."

"I know, Mac." Peggy was standing near us, and when we were alone for a minute, she asked, "Did you notice that?"

"Yes. He seems to be so careful not to hurt our feelings."

"Seems to me it's more than that. He was always considerate. I wondered. Do you think maybe the difference is he doesn't know anymore whether he's hurting your feelings or not?" A little tingle went up my spine. "Maybe," I said, "he can't tell anymore what anybody feels!"

"It could be."

"I always thought that the only reason he could do what he did was that he was the one independent man, sort of apart from everybody else. But now he isn't apart from them anymore. They're thinking about him all over the country. Might be like an overloaded electric line that just burns out."

"I wonder," Peggy said.

The broadcast was early, seven o'clock, and it would be repeated by record-ing for the West Coast later on. After the late afternoon rehearsal, we returned to Colt's new apartment for cocktails. We decided not to eat dinner till after the broadcast. Colt's place was very fancy. Big rooms, huge windows, new modern furniture, and even a television screen built into the wall. I'd moved in tempo-rarily until Peggy and I could be married in the spring.

It was just ten days before Christmas. Outside the snow was falling gently, and inside we were sitting around on foam rubber and plywood, drinking mar-tinis that were mixed by Colt's West Indian houseboy. All but Mac, who had his beer.

"To the Certified Amateur Hour!" said Colt happily. This was what he had worked for: the arithmetic sum of Idea plus Angle.

Miss Lollipop Smith raised her glass and swung a beautiful leg. "And," she said, "to certified literature and art--certified, pasteurized, and homogenized!"

"Cynicism will get you nowhere, Loll," said Colt.

SEX MACHINE

"Are you all right, Uncle Mac?" asked Peggy, probably noticing that he wasn't even looking at Miss Smith's legs.

"Just thinkin', kiddy, just thinkin',"

He was still thinking while we drove down to the studio in a taxi, down Fifth Avenue past the Christmas windows, through crowds of people with colored bundles. The snow was still falling, and every building was lit up from top to bottom. Under these conditions, New York creates the illusion of being a beautiful city.

"Breath taking, isn't it?" asked Peggy. "No matter how long I live here, I'll never get used to it when it's like this!"

"It's a good trick," said Lollipop Smith, "even if it is an atrocious example of the lack of city planning."

"What do you think, Mac?" asked Colt.

"Ummmmm? Think about what, sonny?"

We sat in the clients' room, a plush-lined little cave overlooking the stage, with a soundproof double-glass window, from floor to ceiling. It contained a speaker, and a monitor screen for the television picture. Portal was there, too, along with a few retainers, and so was Mrs. Hipple, the No-Swette lady. She was quite fat and had a sad, drooping, cowlike face. A mink coat hung from her shoulders, and she carried a handbag about the size of a steamer trunk, on which the signs of the zodiac were emblazoned. Bascomb, who fancied himself a television director, was below us in the control room, making life miserable for the man he'd hired to do the actual direction.

Mac, of course, was down on the stage. He had refused to wear a turban, a witch's hat, or sorcerer's robes, and we compromised by seating him behind a large crystal ball. This had an added advantage in television. The camera could zoom in on the ball till it filled the whole screen, then you could super impose on this the image from another camera. That way, you got a sort of double exposure, and it looked as though the super-imposed picture—say, the head of a contestant—were floating in the crystal ball.

From the very beginning of the program (MEDIUM SHOT, CHORUS OF ANGELS: "Has love and romance blessed you yet? Don't risk offending- Use No-Swette!"), I kept my eyes on Mac. He didn't have a great deal to do. The master of ceremonies, a jolly, charming, loveable character, did most of the talking.

"And now, for the Certified Amateur Hour's next contestant, Victor MacInnes will look again in his crystal ball and tell you the one America chooses!" Fanfare. "Who is it, Victor?"

Mac would say, "America chooses Lola Jones!" While the emcee whipped up the applause, the television camera paned down from Mac to the crystal ball, which appeared to contain Lola Jones's head.

Mac did his part as rehearsed, down to the last five minutes. He did have a peculiar, trancelike quality, but we all put that down to nervousness, and the audience no doubt thought it was part of the act. About five minutes before the end of the program, the master of ceremonies announced that the time had come for the great MacInnes to pick the winner, to balance the applause of the studio audience against the verdict of you, and you in the radio audience. After that, the winner was supposed to come on and do an encore.

"Whose face," bubbled the emcee, "do you see in your crystal ball?"

"Sonny," Mac said, "do you figure it's gonna make any difference to the folks sittin' here, or the ones sittin' at home, to know whether the one they like is the same as the one most people like; You figure it's gonna make 'em enjoy the show any more?"

Portal was on his feet. We'd all been to rehearsals, and everybody knew Mac was off the script. "Have them fade him," Portal said, reaching for the phone connected to the control room.

"I'll go down, " Colt shouted, already at the soundproof door.

"Don't you dare." Everybody looked around. It was the sponsor, Mrs. Hipple. "Don't stop him," she said. "He's a Gemini."

"Is that good?" asked Portal.

"It certainly is today!" she said.

Portal shrugged his shoulders and sat down. So did Colt. Mac hadn't stopped. "Nosir," he went on, "I don't think it would. In fact, I've been thinkin' a lot about the whole idea of polls. Maybe you say, right off, 'What's wrong with askin' people what they want, and then givin' it to 'em?' Like votin', isn't it? Is votin' wrong? Nosir, I don't think so. Talk about things gettin' set, and rigid-you watch any country that stops votin' and see how set and rigid they get! Nosir, you vote for a man, not just for the ideas in his head on election day. You vote for him partly because he's the best man you know to step out front, figurin' things out as he goes along. And he knows if he doesn't figure 'em out right, you won't vote for him next time. Now that's all well and good.

"But you take me, or you take any man with a poll. Once you start dependin' on him to tell how to write programs, or books, or anything, why you stop the most important thing before it gets started. And that's ideas, the little germ ideas that grow into all the thoughts, good and bad, that anybody has.

"Why, this system we're startin' now is like sayin' you don't like a tree before you even seen the shape of the seed. We're stoppin' ideas before they get a chance to grow, and we're cuttin' ourselves off from somethin' that's as much our rights as well, as air and sunshine.

"'Course you'd say that you, settin' out there, never asked for this system; you never asked to have people takin' your pulse and askin' you questions. No-sir, it wasn't your fault. It was a lot of mighty smart fellows, and I bet even those fellows thought at first they were doin' a good thing.

"I don't know what we ought to do about it, but you people are goin' to have to work out a way. For one thing, you might try waitin' till things are finished before you call for a vote. More than that, maybe. You might wait till a thing's had a chance to catch on and grow. Maybe have a growin' season for ideas, like we do for seeds and little fishes."

Colt had sunk deeply into his chair. "He's cutting his throat," I heard him mumble. At the same time, the master of ceremonies, who was stunned (and much less jolly and roly-poly) tried to counter-attack.

"Ladies and gentlemen," he began "we'll continue the program with " He was floundering badly.

"You can have the floor in a minute, sonny," Mac said. "Maybe you folks all wonder why I'm sayin' this, and kickin' away a million dollars. Well, wish I could have done it when it did mean sayin' no to all that money. Couldn't do it. Guess I like money too much. That was my weakness. But right now, don't give me cred-it for being noble because I'm not. All of you thinkin' about me gave me kind of a mental short circuit, and I just can't feel anymore what you're all thinkin'.

"Gettin' so I can't feel much of anything any more." He swayed a bit and sat down.

The orchestra started playing loud and fast. A few people in the audience tried to clap, but most of them seemed puzzled as though they thought it might be part of the act, but they couldn't quite see how. A few minutes later our air time was over. Colt stayed behind, trying to talk to Bascomb, trying to find some new angles. Peggy and I ran downstairs, and before anyone could get to him, we reached Mac and hustled him out to an elevator.

Outside, in the Plaza, the snow was still falling, adding real white to the fake snow on the Christmas tree. And on the ice, skaters were spinning about grace-fully in Mr. Rockefeller's moonlight. "Mighty pretty, sonny," said Mac. He looked tired and washed out, but he looked peaceful, too, more so than I'd ever seen him.

"Mighty pretty, Mac," I said. Peggy smiled. And inside me, those little voices didn't say a thing. Not a thing.

Well, right now, Peggy and I are in our house. We had to leave out the guest room, and the study, and the other fireplace, but we did build it. We were married just before we moved We still have a pretty good income, too, thanks to Colt's far reaching deals. Manners' book is number one on the best-seller list, and our share of the royalties is considerable. The second book, even though it's almost identical, has also sold to the movies. And, of course, Slade is still rolling along, coast to coast.

To replace Mac, he and Meacham hired a high-priced stable of writers. They specialize in Hollywood gossip and Red Scares. And we're still getting our cut of Miss Lana Lindie's sizeable Hollywood salary.

Colt isn't satisfied. Television's the thing now, he says, and he has a neat package show all worked out. All he tells me is that it's a gimmick with an angle. If he sells it, he says, it'll make a million. Mac's out here now, spending the weekend with us. He's sitting by the television set, drinking beer and smoking Bull Durham.

"How do you like the show, Mac?" I asked him just now.

"Fair enough, sonny. I go for the little gal with the high voice. But you know, they don't seem to. They like the boy."

"They?" asked Peggy, looking up.

"You know," said Mac, "nobody's thought about me for months."

"You can do it again?" I asked.

Mac just looked at me out of the top of his eyes. "Don't you tell Colt, sonny," he said.

"No, Mac, I won't," I promised. "Never in the world."

"Amen," said Peggy. And besides, I thought, it wouldn't make any difference. Only yesterday, I was reading in the paper that somebody invented a new system. It's very complicated, works by short wave, and radar, and a panel of a thousand people, a perfect cross section of the whole United States. A syndicate was behind it, and according to their spokesman, they could get a nationwide reaction to anything in half an hour flat. I knew it would come. It looked as though they'd duplicated MacInnes—by machine.

OUR OTHER BOOKS

SATAN WAS A LESBIAN

The book that launched a thousand t-shirts is another novel from the pulp era whose title seems to inspire sales without really reflecting the story within. Very cool cover art in our newly restored format. Available at Amazon, eBay and on our own website.

A PICTURE PERFECT AFFAIR

From our sister company The Hotwife Club Press comes a modern bit of erotica. A Picture Perfect Affair tells the story of a boudoir photography session gone sideways and the start of a new lifestyle. This is a novelette that include AI generated images for your enjoyment. Also available as an e Book.

HANGOUT FOR QUEERS

Not what you would expect from the book title, there are no actual queers or looks at queer life in the book. Instead this is a pretty standard sleeze book with our standard of restored cover art and AI generated illustrations.

ISBN 978-1-59362-324-1